"See anything that interests you?" Holt had asked when she'd accidentally bumped into him coming from the bathroom after a shower.

Cory had dragged her gaze to his face and retorted, "You don't have anything I haven't seen before." But she'd lied.

The man was gorgeous. Seated on her sofa, dressed in tight jeans and white western-style shirt, he was irresistible. He glanced up from the book he was reading and smiled—an "I-know-exactly-what-you're-thinking" smile—and she quickly looked away. Then she looked back and he caught her, his black eyes taunting her, stroking her. Desire hung in the air between them like a dense tangle of electrical wires after a storm. When she could stand it no longer, she closed her eyes.

"Cory, I want you."

"I figured as much."

His low, sexy chuckle rippled over her like an aphrodisiac. "Bright lady."

"How about a walk instead? Or some hot chocolate?"

He shook his head.

"A cold shower?"

"Nope," he [illegible] than my share recen[illegible] [illegible]ing his eyes off her, [illegible] is waistband.

"W[illegible] nervously.

Hol[illegible] close for comfort. "Takin[illegible] you that I don't wear it *everyu*[illegible]."

WHAT ARE *LOVESWEPT* ROMANCES?

They are stories of true romance and touching emotion. We believe those two very important ingredients are constants in our highly sensual and very believable stories in the *LOVESWEPT* line. Our goal is to give you, the reader, stories of consistently high quality that may sometimes make you laugh, sometimes make you cry, but are always fresh and creative and contain many delightful surprises within their pages.

Most romance fans read an enormous number of books. Those they truly love, they keep. Others may be traded with friends and soon forgotten. We hope that each *LOVESWEPT* romance will be a treasure—a "keeper." We will always try to publish

LOVE STORIES YOU'LL NEVER FORGET
BY AUTHORS YOU'LL ALWAYS REMEMBER

The Editors

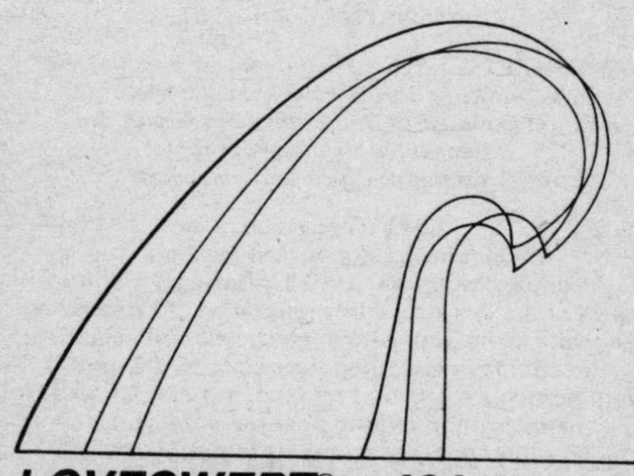

LOVESWEPT® • 464

Jan Hudson

Big and Bright

BANTAM BOOKS
NEW YORK • TORONTO • LONDON • SYDNEY • AUCKLAND

BIG AND BRIGHT

A Bantam Book / April 1991

If you would be interested in receiving protective vinyl covers for your Loveswept books, please write to this address for information:

Loveswept
Bantam Books
P.O. Box 985
Hicksville, NY 11802

ISBN 0-553-44088-8

Published simultaneously in the United States and Canada

Bantam Books are published by Bantam Books, a division of Bantam Doubleday Dell Publishing Group, Inc. Its trademark, consisting of the words "Bantam Books" and the portrayal of a rooster, is Registered in U.S. Patent and Trademark Office and in other countries. Marca Registrada. Bantam Books, 666 Fifth Avenue, New York, New York 10103.

PRINTED IN THE UNITED STATES OF AMERICA

OPM 0 9 8 7 6 5 4 3 2 1

For the members of the
Northwest Houston Chapter
of Romance Writers of America
with love and appreciation.

Special thanks to Captain Bob Prince
and Sergeant Don Morris, Company A,
Texas Rangers.

BIG AND BRIGHT

One

The urge had been coming on her since seven o'clock. Cory Bright had done everything she could think of to shake the feeling, but it wouldn't go away. The obsession loomed in her mind, taunting, compelling. A familiar, distinctive hunger gnawed at her stomach, tightened her chest, and set her throat to aching.

No, she told herself, *I'm not going to give in to this thing.*

She grabbed the home-permanent box and headed for the bathroom in the small apartment overburdened with antiques, antimacassars, and ruffles. Even in the bedroom, cute little samplers, baskets of dried flowers festooned with bits of lace and satin bows, shells filled with her godmother's special blend of herbal soaps, and other ornamental doodads filled every available space. A mélange of scents permeated the rooms: Lilac, lemon, patchouli, sandalwood, strawberry, coconut, vanilla, and pine. And those were just the ones she could identify. There must have been a couple of dozen others wafting up the stairwell from the shop below, insinuating themselves in the Oriental rugs and fringed draperies.

Even though this whole shebang was hers now, the long, narrow flat on Austin's historic Sixth Street was a far cry from her usual surroundings in Atlanta. Cory was a soft leather and Plexiglas person herself. And the only thing her apartment usually smelled of was burnt toast overlaid with a dash of room deodorizer. Oh, well, she thought, she shouldn't look a gift horse in the mouth. And living there was only temporary. In a couple of months, she'd have found a buyer for the shop, then it was on to big-time wheeling and dealing in California. She could hardly wait.

The urge she'd been staving off picked at her again, hounded her, but she pushed it out of her mind, telling herself that it persisted only because she was alone and lonely in a strange town.

By the time the last rod was wound around her long, fine hair, it was nearing midnight. With each tick of the ornate mantel clock, the gnawing grew stronger. She ignored the feeling, squirted foul-smelling solution on the fat curlers, and covered her head with a plastic bag that had held the oranges she'd bought earlier. She read the directions again and checked her watch. Thirty minutes for a body wave.

The clock began to chime the hour. Restless, the urge growing stronger, Cory strode through the living room and into the kitchen. She prowled through the cupboards and frowned at the limited choices. Oat bran wasn't what she craved. Rice cakes wouldn't cut it. She opened the refrigerator and hung one arm on the door as she surveyed the meager fare.

She didn't want a pickle. Or chutney. Or another orange. She tried the cupboard again. Sunflower seeds? No. Raisins? Banana chips? She made a disgusted face. Had her godmother really eaten this stuff?

Only chocolate would do, big, fat chocolate cookies. And they had to have marshmallow in the middle. It had to be a Moon Pie. She'd wanted one since she'd spied a box of them in a grocery store when she bought the oranges and her TV dinner earlier in the evening. Maybe it was because somewhere in her unconscious she associated Moon Pies with comfort and security and childhood. Regardless, she was *dying* for one.

"Oh, hell's bells," she muttered. "I deserve it."

If she hurried, she could run to the all-night store down the block and be back before it was time to neutralize her perm. She pulled on a matching long-tailed shirt over her purple shorts and tank top, tied it at the waist, and grabbed her purse. As an afterthought, she crammed one of Mignon's fancy satin and lace mobcaps over the plastic orange sack on her head, laughing at the sop to her vanity. Except for Mignon Wilson—no, Mignon Marseau now—and Barbara Riley who ran the shop downstairs, she didn't know another soul in Austin, Texas. Barbara was snug in her bed, and Mignon was thousands of miles away in her honeymoon chateau with her little French winemaker.

Since it was Sunday night, the downtown streets were practically deserted. Being out alone felt a little creepy, but Cory's craving overrode caution and prodded her on. The store was less than half a block away. What could happen?

Two minutes later, she shoved open the door of the convenience mart. The sleepy-eyed clerk barely gave her a glance. His nose was stuck in one of those exploitive magazines—the kind they kept behind the counter and sold to pimple-faced boys and macho types who believed that ogling nude women in unnatural poses confirmed their masculinity. Busy reading the stimulating articles, no doubt, she thought.

She strode to the shelves where the cookies were displayed and searched for the box she wanted. Finally spying it in a little nook, she bent over and reached for the last Moon Pie in the carton. Another hand reached in at the same time. It was a big hand, tanned, with long fingers that had blunt tips and neatly trimmed nails.

Both of them grabbed the Moon Pie and neither of them let go. Cory's thumb sank into the edge of the soft pie as she held onto her prize. This was *hers*, dammit. She straightened, swiped back the deep ruffle of her satin cap, and glared up at her opponent. And up. And up.

He must have been six feet six. And the white cowboy hat pulled low on his forehead added another few inches. Except for his white shirt, he was dressed in gray from his eelskin boots to the wide shoulders of his Western-cut suit.

Like everything else about him, his features were large and bold. He had a strong, square chin with a slight cleft, and his high cheekbones, imposing nose, and dark coloring hinted of a Cherokee or Comanche ancestor or two. The eyes meeting hers from under thick, dark brows were sin-black. He was handsome, she supposed, to a woman attracted by the desperado sort who looked like he'd been carved out of a big hunk of walnut with a chain saw. She wasn't that woman.

And this drugstore cowboy with the silver belt buckle that would rival the grill of her car wasn't getting her Moon Pie, no matter how big he was. His piercing gaze flicking over her might turn another woman to mush, but she was immune to his sort. Her thumb dug deeper, and she gave the cellophane package a tug.

The lines at the corners of his eyes crinkled, and his mouth parted in a broad smile that showed a lot of movie-star teeth and deepened the brackets creasing his cheeks.

"Well, ma'am," he said, "it looks like we got us a standoff." His voice was a rumbling bass that resonated from his chest and tingled her toes.

Cory went warm all over. Something about him affected her in a most peculiar way. Maybe it was his size. But even if he did have a good ten inches and a hundred pounds on her, she wasn't going to knuckle under to this bozo. Growing up with four rowdy, obnoxious older brothers had taught her to stick up for her rights.

"*We* got nothing, pardner. This Moon Pie is *mine*." Without batting a lash, she glowered up at those flinty eyes, thrust out her chin, and held on.

He didn't let go either. Instead he stared at her

for a moment with a bewildered expression. "They're purple."

She frowned. Had he slipped a gear? "Huh?"

"Your eyes. They're the same color as my mama's prize pansies. They're the biggest, prettiest purple I've ever seen."

Keeping a straight face, she muttered a terse, "Thank you." She looked down at the mangled package they both still gripped, then back up at him. "The shade is called violet, not purple. But the color of my eyes is not the issue here. Are you going to let go of my Moon Pie?"

"Maybe we could split it over a cup of coffee." His drawl was deep and low and blatantly provocative.

For a half second, she almost considered it. He was, after all, a very attractive man. But then, so was Ted Bundy. And she knew enough about Sixth Street to know that some weird types were attracted to the area. Sixth Street was Austin's equivalent to Bourbon Street in New Orleans. Anyway, this big cowboy was definitely *not* her type. She preferred a gentler, less obvious kind of man. "Look, Tex, I don't know you from Adam, and I'm in a hurry. I'm sharing nothing."

"Holt."

"Pardon?"

"My name is Holt, not Tex. Holt Berringer."

"I don't care if your name is George Bush. This is my Moon Pie, and my hair is curling even as we speak. I have to go."

He laughed and let his gaze trail over her suggestively. "You've put a few kinks in my hair too."

"That tears it!" Cory grabbed the package with both hands and yanked as hard as she could.

Letting go, he held up his hands in a gesture of surrender. The momentum of her tug overbalanced her, and, arms flailing, she thumped down on her bottom. Knocked askew, her mobcap slid down over her eyebrows. Derriere smarting, she clenched her teeth and started counting.

He lifted the frilly ruffle of her cap. "Are you hurt?"

To conceal her humiliation, she glared at the man squatting beside her. His teasing expression had fled, and, to give him credit, he seemed genuinely concerned.

"I'm fine." She pushed the elastic higher on her forehead. "Go away."

"Let me help you up."

When he reached for her, she batted his hand away.

"You're a fractious little filly," he said, his grin returning. "Sure you're not hurt?"

"I'm positive."

He leaned toward her and sniffed. "What's that god-awful smell?"

"The permanent-wave solution on my hair, not that it's any of your business. And it's extremely rude of you to ask."

He only gave her another one of those possum-eating grins. She wanted to brain him. This man had the sensitivity of a bowling ball. He unfolded his six and a half feet of swaggering brawn and again offered his hand. She hesitated, then took it. She was halfway up when, suddenly, he sprawled on the floor and yanked her down beside him.

Her eyes grew large. "Just what do you think—"

"Shhh," he hissed.

"You're bonkers, mister," she hissed back. "You can have the damned Moon Pie. I'd rather have a candy bar." She tried to scoot away and rise to her knees.

He put his palm on her rear end and shoved her back to the floor. "Stay down. Stay quiet. And stay here," he whispered.

He flipped open his coat and drew out a gun. Cory sucked in her breath and swallowed a scream as time and place seemed to shift into slow motion. The iridescent blue-white of the store lights glinted off the big, ugly pearl-handled weapon in his hand. The drone of refrigeration units mingled with the mumble of distant voices and the hum of fluorescent bulbs, becoming a loud buzzing in her ears. The smell of disinfectant on the floor mixed with scents of coffee and popcorn and bug spray and perm solution assailed her nose and turned her stomach. She tried to speak, but her throat was paralyzed and her lips wouldn't move.

This was IT. A crazed cowboy was about to blast her to kingdom come in a convenience store. All she could think of was that her hair was going to be a frizzy mess for her funeral.

She squeezed her eyes shut and waited.

When nothing happened, she opened one eye very slowly. He was gone! Her paralysis vanished. She jumped up, let out a bloodcurdling scream, and dashed for the door.

She came to an abrupt halt and her heart almost stopped when she saw the two men standing at the front counter. They wore Halloween masks. One had a pink pig's face; the other resembled King Kong. The taller, pig-masked one pointed a gun at the ashen-faced cashier, who held his trembling hands over his head.

A holdup! Why me, Lord? Cory spun and bolted.

King Kong grabbed her and dragged her back. "Where do you think you're going?" he growled in her face. His sour breath smelled of onions and beer.

"Don't mind me," she squeaked. "I just came in to buy a Moon Pie. Go right ahead with your business."

The pig held out a paper bag to the clerk. "Put all the money in here."

The frightened man's eyes rolled up, and he slumped to the floor in a dead faint. Pig Face cursed and started around the counter.

"Texas Rangers!" a deep voice shouted from behind the cereal boxes. "Lay down your weapons and put your hands in the air."

Porky Pig dropped to the floor, yanked off his mask, and fired twice into the cornflakes. Boxes and bottles exploded and cereal pelted the aisles. Gorilla Face grabbed Cory by the neck and clutched her in front of him.

"You drop it, Ranger," her captor said, "or I'm going to blow this broad's head off."

Silence.

King Kong was bluffing, Cory thought.

Wasn't he?

He didn't have a gun.

Did he?

"Get to the car, Skeet," the robber gripping her throat said. "We'll be right behind you. He won't risk shooting the dame."

Cory struggled in his grip. "You can't take me hostage!"

"Shut up," he said, tightening his hold.

"But—"

"Shut up, lady!"

Using her as a shield, the robber backed toward the door. Suddenly, Cory was furious. Bloody, blinding furious! How dare this yo-yo try to drag her off with him. She was *not* going to be led meekly away.

Like Popeye after downing a can of spinach, she exploded into action as adrenaline shot through her. She stomped his instep, rammed a sharp elbow into his middle, and twisted from his grip. Whirling, she grabbed a jar of peaches to defend herself. Shots rang out as he lunged for her, and blood blossomed on his shoulder as he spun and toppled. When his gun skittered across the floor, Cory felt distinctly queasy.

"You okay?" Holt yelled as he ran to the door.

"Yes," she called.

She heard the squeal of tires and gunfire as a car roared away. Holt stalked back inside, looking disgusted.

"He got away," Holt said. "And I couldn't even go after him. My car's in a garage a block from here." With the toe of his boot, he rolled King Kong onto his back. "This one's not going anywhere for a while. Will you be all right while I call for help?"

She nodded.

While Holt was on the phone, the onion-breathed ape groaned and tried to sit up. Cory bopped him on the head with the jar of peaches, and he flopped back on the floor. She grabbed two packages of panty hose, tied his wrists and ankles, then slowly slid down the counter to sit on the floor.

Her arms crossed over her knees, she dropped her forehead down. Feeling curlers clunk, she instantly shot her head back up. Her hands flew to her hair. She looked at her watch and gasped. Her permanent! She jumped to her feet and ran for the door.

Holt grabbed her. "Where are you going?"

"I have to go home."

"You can't leave the scene of a crime."

"But you don't understand. It's an emergency. I have to put neutralizer on my hair."

He looked at her as if she were demented. "You can't leave yet. The local police will be here in a couple of minutes."

"But a couple of minutes will be too late. I'll have a head full of corkscrews."

"I'm sorry, but you can't leave."

"Ohhhh . . . damn!" She clenched her teeth and pulled her face into an ugly grimace.

After she thought for a moment, she marched over to the aisle where cosmetics were displayed and scoured the shelves until she found a permanent kit. It wasn't the kind she'd used, but it would have to do. She plunked it down on the counter, grabbed a roll of paper towels, and stomped to the back of the store.

"I'm just going to find some water," she announced over her shoulder.

She moved a mop out of the utility sink and stuck her head under the faucet. When she'd washed out the solution, she blotted the dripping curlers with paper towels and marched back to the counter. In the distance, she heard the wail of sirens.

The clerk, looking glassy-eyed and stunned, sat on a stool. Holt was questioning him.

Cory felt a bit guilty that she'd forgotten all about the cashier. "Are you hurt?" she asked the young man.

"No, I don't think so." He rubbed his head. "I guess I sorta blanked out."

"I'm glad you're okay." She picked up the kit and took out the neutralizer. After snipping off the tip of the applicator nozzle with a pair of fingernail clippers she took from a display on the counter, she thrust the bottle at Holt. "You'll have to help."

Holt looked at the bottle in his hand, then back at the saucy little bundle standing toe-to-toe with him. Her chin jutted defiantly and her eyes flashed like neon. She was a pretty thing, even with that chaos of pink curlers in her hair. Long, sleek legs that wouldn't quit, a nicely curved figure, a full, kissable mouth. But the mouth thinned as he watched it, and her purple—no, *violet*—eyes narrowed beneath a sweep of long, dark lashes.

She tapped her foot and arched one dark eyebrow. "Are you going to help or not, cowboy?"

"Yes, ma'am. What do I do?"

"Pretend that's an oil can. Draw the nozzle along each curl until it's dripping." She turned her back.

Holt bit back a chuckle and went to work, stopping only long enough to identify himself to the paramedics and direct them to the man trussed up with panty hose. He finished his task just as a pair of young patrolmen ran in.

He handed her the empty bottle. "How's that?" he asked.

She patted the curlers in several places. "Fine. Thank you." She cocked her head and looked up at him. "Are you really a Texas Ranger?"

"Yes, ma'am." He pulled his coat back to show her the distinctive silver star pinned to his shirt.

"I thought they went out with train robbers and trail drives and Indian uprisings."

He laughed. "There are still nearly a hundred of us left around to cover the state."

The clerk was so strung out, he couldn't put two coherent words together, so Holt and Ms. Cory Bright, as she identified herself to the officer, related the events to the policemen. Holt had to hand it to Cory. She was as cool as spring water while she recounted her story. He noticed that her hands shook a little and she stopped to draw a couple of deep breaths, but, considering the circumstances, she was calm, and her words were slow and articulate. Most women—hell, most men too—would have been rattled after the ordeal she'd been through. His admiration of her went up another notch.

"Neither of you can identify the second man?" one of the officers asked.

"He wore a Halloween mask," Holt told him.

"*I* saw his face," Cory said. "He pulled off his mask when he started shooting. So that he could see better, I suppose."

They stepped back so that the paramedics could carry the stretcher to the ambulance, then she continued. "He was in his late twenties, I'd say, with brown hair, thinning slightly in front, and hazel eyes. I'd estimate his height to be about six one and his weight about one eighty-five. He had a round face, a pug nose, and a V-shaped scar in the middle of his left eyebrow. And his partner there"—she pointed to the exiting stretcher—" called him Skeet."

Holt's brows shot up. "You're very perceptive."

She shrugged. "I planned to be an artist at one time. I think I can draw a good sketch of him if you'd like."

"That would be a good idea, ma'am," the officer said. "Either of you see the car they drove?"

Holt nodded. "A blue BMW with Georgia plates." He recited the license number.

"But that's *my* car," Cory exclaimed. "That creep stole my car!"

"You leave it unlocked?" Holt asked.

"Certainly not! Do you think I'm crazy? It was locked and parked right in front of Mignon's shop." She slapped her forehead and turned in a circle. "This is unreal. Tell me I'm dreaming. He stole my car!"

"We'll put out a report right away, Ms. Bright. He won't get far unless he ditches the automobile." The officer took her address and phone number, then closed his pad. "Your description is very helpful, ma'am. These two may have been the same ones that hit three other places around town tonight. Killed two people over on the east side."

Killed two people? Cory repeated silently. The reality of the situation hit her, and she felt her knees go weak. She turned and walked very slowly back to the aisle where her purse lay. Reaching to retrieve it, she noticed the smushed Moon Pie on the floor. Her craving had totally disappeared. All she wanted to do was get in bed and pull the covers over her head. What a day.

She picked up her shoulder bag and returned to where the men stood talking. "May I leave now?"

"Who's gonna pay for this stuff?" the clerk asked, nodding toward the permanent kit and the roll of paper towels.

Incredulous, Cory stared at him.

Holt slipped a bill from his money clip and slapped it on the counter. "That should about cover it, buddy." He took Cory's elbow, smiled down at her, and said gently, "I'll see that you get home safely."

His touch, his smile, his nearness sparked a funny tightening in her chest. An irrational part of her wanted to cling to his solid arm and flutter her eyelashes. The feeling, totally out of character for her, was confusing. Blatant machismo such as he exuded was *not* attractive, she reminded herself. And she *never* did anything so silly as flutter her eyelashes. Sexually stereotyped games turned her off.

"Thank you, but you don't need to take me home," she said. "I'm only a few doors away."

"I'll see you home. You don't have any business out alone at this time of night."

"And I suppose *you* do?"

"I'm a man."

Her jaw dropped. She was not believing this. He sounded like a clone of her male chauvinist father and brothers. She tried to think of an effective rejoinder, but all she could do was sputter as he led her to the door.

"Which way?" he asked.

"I am perfectly capable of seeing myself home. Why don't you run along and hand out some speeding tickets or something."

She tried to pull away, but he looped her arm through his and patted her hand. "Texas Rangers don't give out speeding tickets. Those fellows are state highway patrolmen. A Ranger handles major felony investigations—murder, serial killers, organized crime, cattle rustling, gunrunning, and"—he chuckled and rubbed the side of his nose—"a riot now and then."

She frowned. "How did riots get in there?"

He grinned. "Part of the Ranger lore about their toughness. Seems that back in the old days the mayor of one of the towns was expecting trouble, and he wired for help from the Rangers. When only one man with a silver star showed up, the mayor wanted to know where the others were. His answer was something to the effect that it only takes one Ranger to handle one riot."

She made a derisive sound. "Okay, so Rangers are tough guys. But I'm no shrinking violet myself. I'll be just fine on my own."

He patted her hand again. "Humor me, Cory. I'll sleep much better tonight knowing that you're safe and your doors are locked."

She would have argued, but she was simply too tired. She'd only been in Austin twelve hours, and already she'd had a showdown with a Texas Ranger, been in a shoot-out only a few blocks from the state capitol building, and had her BMW—which wasn't even paid for—stolen. And her hair was probably a total disaster. Damn!

Two

A small crowd had gathered outside the store. An odd mixture of street people and passersby craned their necks for a glimpse inside. A gangly young man with carrot-colored hair jockeyed for position, trying to ease past the policeman stationed at the door. A camera hung around his neck, and he carried a notebook.

When Holt and Cory came out the door, he snapped a picture and chased after them. "I'm with the press. Did you see what happened?"

"Can't help you a bit, son," Holt said, never breaking stride. "We just dropped in to buy a Moon Pie."

Looking discouraged, the eager young reporter trotted back to his vigil at the door.

"Why did you lie to him?" Cory asked.

"I didn't lie. Just skirted around the truth. I don't like talking to reporters. They're a pain in the caboose."

Indignant at his attitude, she stopped and looked up at him. "Don't you believe in freedom of the press?"

"Sure I do. Long as they don't get in the way. But I've seen more than one case screwed up by some hot-to-trot reporter. Most of them are nothing but voyeurs and sensationalists."

"I don't agree with you."

He shrugged and steered her down the street. "That's your right."

"Has anyone ever accused you of being a stubborn, opinionated chauvinist?"

He flashed a broad, white-toothed grin. "Once or twice."

"And it didn't bother you?"

"Nope."

Cory bit back a tart reply and stopped at the darkened alcove leading to the outside stairs to her apartment. She stuck out her hand. "Thank you very much for your help, Mi—" She cocked her head. "Exactly how does one address a Texas Ranger?"

Light from the street lamp illuminated his steely eyes, which softened and crinkled at the corners as he gazed at her. "I'm a sergeant, but I'd prefer it if 'one' addressed me as Holt." He held her hand gently but firmly in his, not releasing it when she moved to do so.

The glint in his eyes and the warmth of his big hand stirred an alarming sensation in the pit of her stomach and across the surface of her skin. "Yes, well, uh, thank you very much, Sergeant Berringer. I doubt that our paths will cross again, but I sincerely appreciate your help." She gave his hand a couple of hearty pumps, then yanked her fingers from his grasp. "Good night."

He only looked amused and stood there, silent as a post planted in concrete. Cory whirled and, chin up, headed into the alcove. After two strides she stumbled over a form sprawled in the shadows of the doorway. She shrieked and flew back to Holt, who was right behind her. Heart hammering, she threw herself against his rock-solid length and clutched him for dear life. His arms closed around her and held her tight.

"A body. There's a body in there," she whispered.

He patted her back and murmured soothing words. "It's probably only a bum sleeping one off."

He tucked her against his side and drew her forward. With the toe of his boot, he nudged the form. "Okay, buddy, time to move along."

The body stirred, and a bleary-eyed, grizzled face scowled up at them. "Let's move it," Holt said sternly. "Find another place to sleep."

As the transient muttered and slunk away, Cory sagged against Holt. His tone turned gentle as he said to her, "Just a freeloader, hon. Come on, let's get you inside."

"I feel like such a fool."

"No need. You've had a rough night."

He took her key and unlocked the door, then led her upstairs and unlocked the apartment. Before they went inside, he glanced toward the steps leading to the third floor. "Anybody live up there?"

"A man named Shad Shapiro. I haven't met him yet, but Mignon mentioned him often in her letters. She seems quite fond of him."

Holt insisted that she stay in the living room while he methodically checked the apartment.

"I don't think there's anything under my bed," she said when he returned.

He smiled. "Never can tell. In this part of town, you need better locks. Or at least you need to activate the alarm system when you go out."

"I was only going to be gone for a minute."

"Sometimes that's all it takes. Have you lived here long?"

She chuckled. "Only since about noon. It seems like a lifetime."

"You're tired. You need to go to bed."

"I am tired, but I'm wide awake." She felt the damp curlers on her head. "And I have to take these things out of my hair. Would you like a cup of coffee?" Now why had she said that? she asked herself. The words had just popped out. He'd given her the perfect exit line, and she'd blown it.

He nodded. "I'll rustle up some while you fix your hair."

In the fussy apartment that smelled like a cross between a perfume factory and a beauty shop, Holt took off his hat and laid it on a table, picking the only bare spot among a bunch of little whatnots. He grinned as he ran his fingers through his hair. Cory Bright didn't seem to fit this place. She didn't seem the type to go in for doilies and dust catchers. Not that he'd figured out exactly what type she was. For the short time he'd been around her, she seemed to be a mess of contradictions. Gutsy and vulnerable. Hard and soft. Spitting tiger and cuddly kitten. He wasn't sure what the real Cory was like, but he was interested in finding out. Mighty interested.

He rummaged around in the kitchen and decided to fix hot chocolate instead of coffee. Since the cupboards and refrigerator were almost bare, he had to use canned milk and forego the marshmallows he preferred. Still it was palatable, he decided, tasting the mixture in the pan.

He was pouring the chocolate into mugs when Cory came in. He stopped, dumbfounded by the sight of her. The only thing that had changed was her hair, but it was dazzling. It swept past her shoulders in a soft, shining cloud the color of clover honey and sweet cream. It made him want to run his fingers through it and rub it against his cheek and feel its silkiness tumbling against his chest.

She ran her hand down one side of her hair and pulled a skein of it over her shoulder. As she toyed with the loose coil, Holt couldn't take his eyes off her long, delicate fingers. She dropped the curl and her hand slipped into the opening of her shirt to rub a spot just under her collarbone. His imagination went wild.

"At least my hair didn't fry as I was afraid it would." She crossed the room and leaned over to smell the contents of the pan. "Oh, good. I love hot chocolate. I wish we had some marshmallows."

Holt couldn't help himself. His hand lifted of its own accord to a tress of her hair. He sifted it through his fingers. It felt as soft and silky as a kitten's fur. "It's beautiful," he said, unable to keep the hoarseness from his voice.

"Thank you." Seeming to be self-conscious, she looked away.

"Shall I go out to get some marshmallows?" he asked.

"Oh, no. This will be fine."

He filled the mugs, and they carried them into the living room. She curled up on the settee, and he took a more substantial-looking easy chair.

After an awkward silence, he asked, "What brought you to Austin?"

She laughed. "My godmother's marriage. Not here. In France. It's a long story."

"I've got time."

She held the mug to her lips and traced the rim with the tip of her tongue. Watching the slow, unconscious action, Holt felt himself growing aroused.

"Mignon, my godmother, was French. She came to the United States just after World War II as a very young bride. Her husband, Frank Wilson, was my mother's cousin. Since there wasn't much to do in Goat Hill, Arkansas, but socialize with the neighbors, Mignon and my mother became close friends. By the time I came along, Mignon and Frank still didn't have children, so she spoiled me rotten. I adored her, and I was devastated when they moved to Austin when I was about fourteen."

As Cory paused to take another sip of hot chocolate, Holt saw a flash of pain in her eyes. She masked it quickly with a smile. "I would have gone with her if I could have. Life in Goat Hill, Arkansas, was the pits. Anyway, Frank died a few years later and Mignon opened a shop selling custom-blended perfumes. Her family had been perfumers before the war. She became very successful and expanded her business by offering a greater variety of merchandise, some mail order, that sort of thing. Her distinctive products are very much in demand."

"Ah," Holt said. "That's what I smell."

Cory smiled. "From the shop downstairs, plus all the scented things up here. They're all Mignon's special ingredients. She's really a genius."

He glanced around the room. "That explains it. This is your godmother's apartment."

"No, I suppose it's mine now."

"You suppose? Did she die?"

Cory laughed. "Hardly. She went to France on a buying trip, ran into her childhood sweetheart, and married him. She's living in grand style with the owner of one of the leading wineries in France. I'm delighted for her."

Puzzled, Holt frowned. "How do you fit in?"

"I was very surprised to receive a letter from Mignon along with papers from her attorney. It seems that she planned to leave everything to me after her death, and 'since Henri came back into my life, cherie,'" Cory quoted in a French accent, "'I feel as eef I have died and gone to heaven.' She signed everything she owned in Austin over to me."

The news pleased him. "So you're going to be around permanently?"

"Gadzooks, no. As soon as I can do an inventory, I'm going to put the place on the market."

His smile faded. "It seems a shame to turn your godmother's business over to a stranger. Obviously, she wanted you to have it."

She shrugged. "Mignon said there were no strings. She even left me her book of formulas, but that sort of stuff might as well be concoctions of eye of newt and frog ears for all I know about it. If Rebecca Snook hadn't been my lab partner, I would have flunked high school chemistry. Advertising is my forte. I'm an account executive and a darned good one. I'd about topped out in Atlanta, so now I have feelers out to some of the big ad agencies in Los Angeles. That's where the action is."

She stifled a yawn. "I can't believe that I've sat here and babbled my whole life story to you. My mother always said I could talk the horns off a billy goat, but my tongue usually isn't quite so loose." Another yawn formed, and she laughed. "I'm even boring myself."

He chuckled. "You're probably having a reaction from all the hoopla tonight. Besides, I like listening to you. I'm not much of a talker myself."

"How did you decide to become a Texas Ranger?"

Holt stood. "I think we'd better save that story for another time. You look sleepy."

She smiled lazily and stretched. "The chocolate did it. Thanks." She rose and walked him to the door.

"I'll pick you up for dinner about seven."

Her chin went up. "Oh, no. I'm afraid I have too much to do."

"You have to eat. We won't go anyplace fancy, and I'll bring you home early."

"I'm sorry, but—"

He touched his finger to her lips. "I thought you wanted to find out how I became a Texas Ranger," he said. It was a story he rarely told strangers, but he hoped to appeal to her good manners. "We'll finish our tales then." He ran the knuckle of his index finger along the edge of her chin, touched the tip of her nose, and left.

The next morning Cory, dressed in khaki slacks and a blue pullover, took her second cup of coffee down the interior stairs to the fragrance-filled shop. Maybe starting to work would keep her mind off Holt Berringer, she mused. For some reason she couldn't fathom, he kept intruding in her thoughts. He might be a prime cut of Texas beef, but she wasn't interested. Nothing about him jibed with her concept of the ideal man.

Through the front glass, she could see Barbara Riley unlocking the door. Cory had met her briefly the day before when she and her husband, John, an engineer with a computer manufacturing company, had met her to deliver the keys. The soft-spoken Englishwoman had worked for Mignon for several years, managing the store and charming customers, Cory was sure, with her droll wit and merry eyes. Besides Barbara, three or four college students worked part-time in odd shifts during afternoons and evenings and on Saturdays.

With a cheery "Good morning," Barbara bustled into the shop, the skirt of her flowered dress swishing about her legs. She was not much more than Cory's thirty-two, a bit on the plump side, and wore her blond hair in an old-fashioned coronet of braids.

"Good morning," Cory replied, smiling. Her steps muffled by thick green carpet, she walked to the front of the store where sunlight spilled through multipaned bay windows, bathing the baskets of ivy and fern hanging in the shallow recesses. The midmorning bustle of traffic outside was a marked contrast to the quiet of yesterday's Sunday streets.

"Have you had time to look about yet?" Barbara asked.

"No, I'm afraid I was a sleepyhead. I've just come down."

Barbara laid a bundle of irises on a beveled glass display case filled with crystal bottles and dainty baskets of sachets, then stowed her purse under the ornate counter which, in an earlier incarnation, had been a bar. "I'm sure you needed the rest. No matter. We've a few minutes before the shop opens. Let me put these in water, and I'll acquaint you with Mignon's Sixth Scents." She retrieved the bundle of long-stemmed purple flowers. "Are you going to change the name of the shop? I suppose you could drop the 'Mignon's' easily enough."

"Oh, I wouldn't change the name."

Cory sipped her coffee as she followed Barbara across the public area. Scattered around it was a quaint mixture of French and Victorian pieces that, except for a few display cases, gave the impression of a large sitting room rather than a business. Cut-glass bowls of scented soaps and votive candles filled wooden risers along an antique brick wall. Apothecary jars of bright-hued substances and clear boxes of potpourri lined the glass shelves of a large étagère that stood against the opposite wall, which was plastered and painted a soft cream.

At the back of the room, Barbara opened a door and flipped on the overhead lights of the workroom, which, along with an office carved out of one corner, took up two-thirds of the long, narrow building. The stark area was a surprising divergence from the shop and its fussy decor. Although it was done in pleasant shades of butter-yellow, mint-green, and white, and framed prints of flowers and herbs lined one wall, the workroom was strictly utilitarian. Work counters were covered in Formica; the floors were cushioned tile; the sinks were stainless steel. Hundreds of labeled bottles stood in neat rows on the shelves. It looked like a laboratory, which, Cory surmised, it was.

While Barbara arranged the irises in a vase, Cory browsed among the bottles, studying the labels at random. She recognized jasmine, rose, and vanilla, but what in the world were bergamot, neroli, and ylang-ylang?

Picking up the thread of their earlier exchange, Cory said, "Since Mignon has built a clientele over the years, it makes sense to keep her name on the business, but I suppose the final decision will rest with the new owner."

Barbara turned, a stricken look on her face. "New owner? But surely you don't mean to *sell* the shop? I assumed . . ." She pressed her lips together and resumed her arrangement of the flowers. After a long pause, she said, "I assumed that you would take Mignon's place."

"Heavens, no." Cory chuckled. "I don't even recognize the names of most of this stuff. All I know about her perfume is that she sent me a big supply every year for Christmas."

"Have you found a buyer yet?"

"No. I thought I would take inventory before I put it on the market. Since you've been here so long, I was thinking you might be interested."

Barbara laughed. "Wouldn't I just. But John and I could never afford it. Mignon's formula book alone is worth hundreds of thousands of dollars."

Cory's sip of coffee went down the wrong way, and she began to cough. She beat on her chest until her breath was restored. "Hundreds of thousands? My Lord! You're kidding me."

"Oh, no. I know of at least two firms who have offered her as much. One from New York, another from London. And her mail-order business has grown so rapidly, she had to move it from here to a warehouse and employ a staff. Many of the items she used to produce here are now subcontracted to a manufacturer in Dallas. Didn't you know?"

Feeling overwhelmed, Cory plunked down on a stool. "Not a clue. But I've only seen Mignon twice in the last six years. Once, just after my divorce when I came to spend two weeks to lick my wounds—her shop was still in her house then—and two years ago, when I went with her to France on a buying trip. Why in the world would she sign all this over to me?"

"Because she loves you very much. You are the daughter she never had. Henri Marseau is extremely wealthy, so she no longer needs the income. Mignon can retire now and enjoy her life with him."

"I'm stunned. I thought Mignon only had a

funky little shop in a touristy part of town. I never dreamed . . ."

Barbara smiled. "It *is* a funky little shop, and Mignon loved Sixth Street. She said the energy and the people reminded her of the Left Bank in Paris. It becomes a bit boisterous around here at night and on the weekends—too energetic for my taste—but she's always been very young at heart."

Cory laughed. "It was a bit boisterous last night." She related her misadventure.

"Oh, my," Barbara said, her eyes wide. "How fortunate that you weren't injured. Do you suppose your car will be recovered?"

"I certainly hope so. Of course it's insured, but I love that car. I saved for a long time to be able to afford it, and I still owe the bank thirteen payments."

Barbara checked her watch. "Ten o'clock. It's time for me to open the shop. Why don't you take a look at Mignon's office? Her accountant is scheduled to drop by this afternoon for a consultation with you. I'm sure she can give you a thorough statement of your assets."

Monday evening Cory rushed around getting dressed, wishing she hadn't allowed herself to be manipulated into dinner with Holt Berringer. She had a lot to think about. Her meeting with Carol Sanders, the accountant, had been mind-boggling. Not only did she now own the shop and its inventory, but also the entire building on Sixth Street, a warehouse, and several other pieces of real estate. Plus, Carol had confirmed that Mignon's formula book, locked in a safe-deposit box at the bank, *was* worth a small fortune. Then there was the matter of Mignon's employees to consider. Cory was now responsible for the livelihood of eight people.

At least, with her newfound wealth, she wouldn't have to worry about her car payments anymore. Quitting her lucrative job in Atlanta to come there had been scary. Not that she'd had any real alternative about finding another job. Things had gotten to a point where either she had to accept Woody Shield's proposal or leave the company. He'd been pressing her to marry him, and she'd been stalling. Her batting average with men hadn't been all that great. Although Woody, who was an artist with the same ad agency she worked for, seemed to have all the qualities she admired in a man, something hadn't been quite right. Coming to Austin had been an excuse to say no without the awkwardness of having to cope with his hangdog expression every day.

She'd been toying with the idea of a career move for several months, anyhow. She needed new challenges. And wouldn't her family just croak, she thought, grinning, if she made it really big in L.A.? Her father and brothers still insisted she needed a man to take care of her. Humph!

She checked her appearance in the cheval mirror, hoping she was appropriately dressed. Since Holt had said "nothing fancy," she'd settled on comfortable yellow knit pants and a matching short-sleeved top. The entire front of the shirt had been appliquéd into a bright turquoise and teal underwater scene with whimsical satin and suede fish highlighted with sequins and swimming among bold fronds of sea plants. It was a fun outfit and one that never failed to boost her spirits. With all the weighty information she'd had dumped on her that day and facing an evening with a man who made her edgy, she needed the fortification.

At precisely seven o'clock, the downstairs buzzer sounded. She pressed the button to unlock the door and waited, listening to the thump of boots climbing the wooden steps. As the measured *thump-thump* grew louder, she could feel her heart beating to the same tempo. The sound seemed ominous, like a portent of something eminently disruptive in her life.

When he knocked, she peered through the tiny viewer in the door and saw Holt, Stetson pulled low over his eyes, jean jacket collar turned up, staring back at her. She'd forgotten how handsome, how bigger than life, how formidable, how *virile* he was. Waves of his essence—very confident, very basic, and very male—seemed to bombard the door and seep through the wood.

One corner of his mouth twitched into a smile, and she jumped back, as startled as if she'd been caught peeping through a keyhole into his bedroom.

She almost refused to open the door.

Don't be silly, she told herself. You've never been attracted to his type. But her hand trembled as she turned the knob. Maybe it was because she'd skipped lunch.

"Hello there," she said, affecting a breezy tone as she swung the door open. "Come in."

He removed his hat and stepped inside. Her

quick glance noted that beneath the denim jacket he wore a red open-necked shirt tucked into tight jeans. The jeans had a knife-edge crease, and the big silver buckle at his waist rode low. His boots were black and well shined.

His perusal of her, however, was not so cursory. His eyes made a lazy trip from crown to toes and back again.

"Nice. Very—" He frowned, then he squinted at her.

"Something wrong?"

"I could have sworn your eyes were violet. Now they look turquoise."

Amused by his consternation, she said, "They tend to change with the colors I wear." She drew her brows together. "Are you wearing your gun tonight?"

"I *always* wear my gun. Except . . . when I'm in bed."

Cory watched, practically mesmerized by his black gaze, as one side of his mouth lifted in a slow smile that deepened the groove along his cheek. "Bed" reverberated in her ears, and images of a solid, tanned body flitted through her head. She had the wildest urge to run her fingers through his thick, dark hair to test if it was coarse or soft.

"Do you mind?" he asked.

"Mind?" She shook herself and lifted her chin. "I'm sure what you do in bed is none of my concern."

He laughed. "I meant, do you mind if I wear my gun? I feel kind of naked without it."

Naked, naked, naked, came the echo. Her eyes widened. She swallowed and shook herself again.

Obviously, low blood sugar was making her light-headed. "No, of course not." After all, having dinner with this macho cowboy was not a habit she was planning to cultivate. "Would you like a drink or shall we go?"

"Go. Parking around here is dang near impossible. I walked over from the hotel while the boy was getting my car from the garage."

"Are you staying in a hotel? I thought you lived in Austin."

"Yep."

"Yep, you're staying in a hotel, or yep, you live in Austin?"

He chuckled. "Both. It's a long story."

"I've got time."

"Now where have I heard that before?"

Cory picked up her bag and, at Holt's insistence, set the alarm before they left. They walked a half block and crossed the street to the Driskill Hotel, a grand building over a hundred years old, according to Holt.

"My house is being overhauled after some fire damage," he explained, "so I'm only staying at the hotel temporarily. I've always loved the place. My great-granddaddy stayed here when it was new. I can almost hear the walls talking."

"So your family has lived in Texas a long time?"

"Six generations. Since long before Texas was a state." He steered her to a silver Lincoln Town Car parked at the curb and helped her in.

The powerful car pulled out into the street, and they were quiet for a moment as he maneuvered through traffic. Confined in the car with him, Cory could feel those waves again. She wiggled in the soft leather seat and searched for something to say to get her mind off the bombardment.

"Have there been any other Texas Rangers in your family?"

"Seven. Five generations of them."

"Only five? What happened to the sixth?"

He glanced over at her and smiled. "My mother was an only child. She couldn't pass the physical."

Cory's spine stiffened. "Can't women be Rangers?"

"Never have been."

She took a deep breath and bit her tongue. Anyone with a brain could see that defending women's rights with this throwback would be an exercise in futility, and she was no dummy. She sighed and began to snap and unsnap her purse. The sound of rapid clicking filled the car.

When they stopped at a traffic light, he glanced at her again. "You ticked off about something?"

"Me? Ticked off? Why, whatever gave you that idea, Sergeant Berringer?" she asked sweetly.

"Your chin's jacked up a good three notches, and you're about to worry that purse to death. Did I say something to rile you?"

"Rile me? Of course not. I'm prone to ignore the mutterings of someone with the intelligence of a flea and the sensitivity of a crookneck squash."

Holt threw back his head and laughed. It was a rich, free guffaw that shook his shoulders and bobbled his Adam's apple. A car behind him honked, and, still laughing, he drove on. He quieted, then another spasm of chuckles burst forth. "A crookneck squash?"

Cory felt her face blaze. "I'm sorry. I shouldn't

have said that. Sometimes my temper gets away with me."

"Hon, always say what you want to say to me, and don't ever apologize for it. I appreciate plain speaking. But I would like to know what set you off."

"Your mother."

"My mother?"

"You said your mother couldn't pass the *physical.*"

"She couldn't. She had polio as a kid. It left her with some damage."

"Oh." She slunk down in the seat, feeling lower than a worm, but determined to vindicate herself. "Why aren't there any women Rangers?"

He shrugged. "I don't know. There never have been. I suppose there may be someday."

"Austin is a very pretty town."

"Yep, I like it." He looked over and grinned. Her abrupt change of subject hadn't fooled him for a minute. "I heard that your car has been recovered."

"Yes. The police called this afternoon and said they found my car abandoned near the airport. I'm supposed to pick it up in the morning."

"I'll take you."

"Oh, no, I wouldn't want to be a bother—"

"No bother. I'm living only a block away, and my schedule tomorrow is flexible."

They pulled into the back lot of the Lakeside Café, a weathered wood restaurant on a sandstone bluff overlooking a blue-green stretch of water. The Colorado River, Holt explained as they walked to the café, formed Lake Travis farther west of town, Lake Austin here, then meandered through the capital city, forming Town Lake on its snaking path to the Gulf of Mexico three hundred miles away.

Following the delicious smells of food, they went down stone steps to the informal room that was built around the trunk of an enormous live oak. The tree, which must have been four or five feet in diameter, rose through the ceiling and its branches spanned the roof.

"Inside or outside?" Holt asked, pointing to tables on a wooden deck shaded by other huge oak branches.

"Outside, please. I've been inside all day."

Once seated, they ordered drinks and sipped them, enjoying the pleasant evening, watching an occasional canoe paddle by and around the bend of the lake. "It's very nice here," Cory said.

"April in Texas is just about perfect," Holt said. "In another month, days will begin to get hotter than a two-dollar pistol."

As they ate dinner, they talked about all sorts of things. Rather, Cory discovered, she did most of the talking. Holt seemed content to watch her and draw her out with casual questions. He was a slick one, she thought. She'd practically spilled her whole life story, and she hardly knew anything about him. When she tried asking questions, he gave a brief reply, then had her babbling again.

And the way he looked at her! She could almost feel the intensity of his gaze wrapping around her like slow-creeping tendrils of a vine, pulling her toward him. At one point, the feeling became so unsettling, she was sure he was trying to hypnotize her with those disquieting black eyes. She squirmed and was relieved when the waitress interrupted the moment by refilling their water glasses.

Near the end of their meal, they watched the sun slide behind tree-covered hills beyond the water. She must have been staring raptly at the sight for he asked, "You like sunsets?"

"I don't think there's anything more beautiful."

"We have a place on Lake Travis that's famous for its sunsets. I'll take you one evening this week."

She brightened. "Wonderful! I'd love to see it."

Now why had she said that? Another encounter with Holt was not in her plans. All the way home she worried about how to renege on her promise gracefully.

When they were back on Sixth Street and her apartment door was open, she asked, "Would you like to come in for coffee?"

Damn! she thought, rolling her eyes. She'd done it again.

His eyes glittered with amusement as if he could read her mind. "Not tonight, but thank you. I promised that this would be an early evening. I'll see you in the morning. Is nine okay?"

"Nine's . . . fine." She realized her voice sounded kind of far-off and dreamy as she stared at his mouth, fascinated by its shape, wondering how it would feel against hers. As if self-directed, her eyelids fluttered and her lips began to tremble and pucker.

"Good night, princess."

She waited.

The door closed.

Three

Cory, breath held and lips still puckered, opened her eyes and stared at the door. For a long time, she stood there, trying to make sense of the disappointment nagging at her, trying to keep from feeling like a fool.

But she did fell like a fool, an absolute nitwit. Why hadn't he kissed her? Unless she'd misread the signals, he'd wanted to. She'd been prepared to deliver a quick, platonic peck herself, to let him know exactly what he could expect from her—nothing but the most casual friendship. No heavy breathing, no groping, no tussles in the sack. But the scoundrel hadn't even given her the chance. Was he abiding by some gallant Ranger code or was he playing a game to keep her off guard? Her eyes narrowed. The latter, she suspected.

Well, Sergeant Holt Berringer was in for a surprise. She wasn't one of those vapid females who went gaga over swaggering sinew and blatant bulges. She'd grown up in a houseful of domineering males who thought that muscles, chest hair, and external plumbing made them superior. Masculine arrogance and barely leashed primitive instincts turned her off.

She preferred men with subtlety and depth, men with tenderness and finesse who weren't afraid to show their emotions, not the strutting peacock variety who knew only wham-bam, thank you, ma'am. She'd had that bitter lesson reinforced as a freshman in college.

Then why, she asked herself, was she still standing there feeling disappointed? Why was she wondering how Holt's lips would feel on hers? Why did her skin tingle when she thought of his hands?

Just as she turned away, someone banged on the door. Allowing herself a slight smirk of feminine satisfaction, she jerked the door open.

But instead of Holt standing there as she expected, another mountain of a man filled the frame. He looked like a grizzly bear in black leather and silver spikes. Tattooed dragons, breathing orange fire, wound around each bare beefy arm. A red bandanna was knotted at his thick neck, and his dark hair, thinning on top and streaked with gray, stood out in frizzy tufts like wads of tree moss stuck to his head. Below his bulbous nose, his broad grin revealed a gaping hole where a lateral incisor and a cuspid had once been.

Letting out a roar that was a cross between a rebel yell and a train whistle, he lunged for her, wrapping his arms around her and lifting her off the floor.

Cory screamed as he swung her around.

"Hot damn, little mama," he boomed, laughing as he swung her around again, "it's about time you showed up. Folks are waitin'. Let's party!"

With her squealing and beating on his massive chest, he swung her around once more and let out another roar.

"Set her down, buddy," a deep voice said from the doorway. "Real easy."

The burly man holding her had his back to the door. He let Cory slide down his girth until her feet touched the floor, then turned, shielding her with his massive bulk. "Who in the hell are you?" he growled.

Cory peeked around his shoulder and gasped as she saw Holt, gun drawn and eyes narrowed to steely slits.

"Holt Berringer, Texas Ranger. Who in the hell are you?"

"So you're Cory's Ranger." The wild man laughed and held out a beefy hand. "I'm her upstairs neighbor, Shadrach. I own the Fiery Furnace down the street."

Holt scowled at the man, then looked to Cory for confirmation. Some perverse sense of devilment kept her from explaining that her upstairs tenant was Shadrach of the Fiery Furnace only by night. By day he was Dr. Shad Shapiro, a music professor at the University of Texas, who looked very different in a necktie. When she nodded, Holt put away his gun and, though he didn't look too happy about it, shook the man's outstretched hand.

"I'm sorry that I made such a commotion, Shad," Cory said, smiling. "For a moment I didn't recognize you in your . . . uh, outfit." To Holt she added, "I met Shad this afternoon. I promised that I'd stop by his club for a drink tonight so I could meet some of my Sixth Street neighbors. It completely slipped my mind."

Holt still didn't look too happy.

She fidgeted with the hem of her shirt, winding the knit fabric around her finger. "Would you like to come with us?"

Eyeing Shad with a wary expression, Holt slowly nodded. Shad only rocked back on his heels and grinned.

The trio had started out the door when a beeper in Holt's pocket went off. "May I use your phone?" he asked.

He disappeared into the kitchen for a few moments, then returned looking grim. "Emergency. I have to leave."

Shad's grin widened. "We'll miss you, man."

Holt ignored him and pulled Cory aside. "I don't want you going off with that character alone. Tell him you'll go another night when I can take you."

Her eyebrows shot up. "I beg your pardon?"

"The crowd that hangs out at the Fiery Furnace is rougher than a three-cornered cob. A woman alone doesn't have any business hanging around that joint."

"I won't be alone. I'm going with Shad."

Holt snorted. "That fruitcake's part of the problem. You need to stay *here* with the door locked and the alarm on."

Her chin rose and she didn't even try to count. "Sergeant Berringer, exactly what gives you the right to think you can butt into my business?" Cold ire frosted her voice as she enunciated each word. "I am reasonably intelligent and have been of legal age for several years. I damned well don't need some puffed-up stud telling me what to do. I'll go *where* I please, *when* I please, and with *whom* I please. Do I make myself clear?"

He sucked in a deep breath, then let it out. "Yes, ma'am, I don't think you could make it any clearer than that." He strode to the door without looking back, and Cory heard the loud clatter of his boots going down the stairs.

Shad chuckled. "Looks like your kicker's got a bad case of the greens."

"Of what?"

"He's jealous."

"That's ridiculous. I only met him last night."

"Maybe so, but that dude acts like he's already staked a claim."

She shook her head. "He's just naturally bossy."

Shad only flashed a snaggletoothed grin. "You ready to meet the crowd?"

After she'd locked up—Shad was as fussy about that as Holt—they went downstairs and headed for the Fiery Furnace two doors away. Five big Harleys were parked outside and rock music blasted from inside. The door was a dark hole edged with painted flames and orange Christmas lights.

Even if Holt hadn't made such a big deal about it, she would have felt a little nervous about going into the place. Shad must have felt her tension, for he tugged her arm.

"Come on in, sweet cakes. We're all friends. The set is about over, and I'll introduce you around."

Cory took a deep breath and plunged into the black cavity. The smoky air smelled like the inside of an old beer keg and the floor was lumpy with peanut shells and cigarette butts.

While her eyes strained to adjust to the darkness and her ears to the assault from the amps, Shad steered her to two tables of bikers and their ladies. She couldn't see much of them—only enough to know that she wouldn't want to meet any one of them alone in a dark alley.

Shad threw one trunklike arm around her neck and pulled her against him. "Cory, meet some of our regulars." He called off a collection of names, but the only ones she remembered were Roscoe, Mugger, and Dimples. They all hoisted their beer bottles to her.

"Cory is gonna be running the smell shop down the street from now on," Shad told them. "She's Minnie's goddaughter. I told Minnie we'd look out for her."

Minnie? Cory couldn't imagine anyone calling Mignon, Minnie. Nor could she imagine her godmother sipping brew with this motley assortment.

"Minnie was a cool lady," Mugger said. "We'll watch out for you, babe."

The others echoed his sentiments with a variety of grunts and thumbs-up. Dimples, a straw-haired blonde in dire need of a root touch-up, stood and stuck out her hand to shake Cory's. Obviously the main squeeze of the biker auxiliary, she had the looks and the grip of a lady mud wrestler. Obscene words on the front of her well-packed tank top jiggled with the movement of her energetic greeting.

"Don't let this bunch spook you." Dimples smiled sweetly, showing the deep indentations in her cheeks that had named her. "We're just regular folks. And we liked Minnie a lot. Welcome to Austin."

"Thanks," Cory said, returning her smile.

With a crescendo of crashing cymbals and squealing synthesizer, the band ended the set and broke. Shad introduced her to the musicians, all his students at the University of Texas. Although Shad's own band played weekends, he brought in new groups that needed experience to play during the week.

"And we work cheap," the long-haired drummer said.

Shad cuffed him playfully, then drew Cory to the bar, where he introduced the two bartenders and a couple of the waitresses. He grabbed one attractive woman carrying a tray of drinks. "And who is this hag?"

The woman laughed. "I'm Marcia Stern," she said to Cory. "Barmaid, ABD in economics, and fiancée of this toothless wild man who takes out his bridge when the sun goes down."

Cory smiled at the affectionate bantering between the two. "What is ABD?"

"'All but dissertation.' I'm a struggling grad student at UT. Let me deliver this round, and I'll take a break."

"She's nice," Cory said to Shad as Marcia headed for a crowded table.

"Ummm." Shad grinned. "How about a drink? You want beer or one of the house specialties? I can give you Steam Heat, Molten Lava, or a Blazing Inferno."

"I'm afraid to ask what's in those things. Keeping in mind that I'm not a two-fisted drinker, you pick something."

He ordered a beer for himself and a Molten Lava for her. "The ladies usually like them," he explained.

She did like the drink. Fruity and refreshing, it was a red slushy concoction with a sliver of dry ice added for a bubbling, smoky effect. While she sipped it, Shad introduced her to a state senator and a governor's aide, as well as two young women in skimpy outfits who'd dropped by the bar to meet her.

"Ming and Tanya work at the Mockingbird Massage Parlor upstairs," he said.

Cory kept a straight face as she greeted the two who, she was sure, had never studied massage therapy in an accredited school.

When the band started again, Shad excused himself for a few minutes to go out on the sidewalk to hawk business. Marcia returned to the bar to order a soda for herself, another Molten Lava for Cory, then the two women wove their way to a small table in the corner.

Marcia slipped off her shoes, propped her feet on a chair, and wiggled her toes. "Boy that feels good. The only bad thing about this job is that it's murder on the tootsies. I'm glad this is a slow night."

A slow night? But the place is almost full."

Business becomes brisker on the street as the week progresses. By Friday night, this place is wall-to-wall bodies. It's a zoo."

"I'm surprised you work here. I would think an economist—"

"Ought to be working in a bank or for one of the government agencies?" Marcia laughed. "The hours don't match my schedule. I'm a graduate assistant during the morning, and I do my research in the afternoons. Besides, with tips, the pay here is better."

Shad must have spread the word, for several people came by to meet Cory. Wee Willie, who sold flowers and balloons on the corner, presented her with a yellow rose; Vance, a restaurant owner from across the street, bought her another Molten Lava and promised a dinner on the house; Sally, who ran a gallery around the corner, invited her to a showing of an up-and-coming artist. Sid, a headliner in one of the comedy clubs, joined them for another drink and quickly had them all laughing. His every rapid-fire utterance was uproariously funny. Cory was having a blast.

When there was a lull in the one-liners and the stream of people dropping by the table, Marcia leaned over and poked her. "Do you know a big, good-looking guy who wears a white cowboy hat and has eyes like a rattlesnake?"

"Why?"

"He's been nursing a beer at the bar for the last half hour and staring a hole through you."

Cory blinked, trying to focus. That last Molten Lava seemed to have affected her vision. Recognizing Holt, she grinned, stuck her arm in the air, and wiggled her fingers. "Yoo-hoo."

Grabbing his long-neck by the throat, he strolled over to the table. She tried to introduce him to Sid and Marcia, but her tongue tangled and her mouth wouldn't work right. She giggled.

"I think it's about time for you to go home," Holt said.

She peered up at him. "Nope. I'm having too much fun." She patted the empty chair beside her. "Sit down. Sid is soooo funny. Isn't he funny, Marcia? Say something funny, Sid."

Holt sat down, draping his arm over the back of her chair, and looked at Sid.

Sid shifted in his seat, gulped some of his drink, shifted again. "Well . . . uh, I guess I'd better get going," he said, rising. "Catch you later." He left in a hurry.

"Ohhh." Cory pouted. "Why did he leave?"

Marcia chuckled.

"It's late," Holt said. "Time to go home."

Cory sighed.

"Let's go," he said, standing and picking up her purse.

When she tried to stand, her legs went rubbery. "Oops." She giggled and plunked back down in her chair.

How many of those things have you had?" Holt asked.

She held up three fingers. "Five."

He pulled her up and slipped his arm around her waist to support her. "Nice to meet you, ma'am," he said to Marcia, tugging the front brim of his hat.

"Need some help?" she asked.

"I can handle it."

Cory's arm swooped out and grabbed the wilting yellow rosebud from the table. She tapped Holt's nose with it. "He can handle anything." She looked at Marcia and said in a stage whisper, "He's a

Texas Ranger, you know. He's very handsome, don't you think? And *very* macho. It's a shame he's not my type. I'll bet he's a stud in bed."

Holt chuckled.

So did Marcia.

"Are you a stud in bed, Holt?" Cory tapped his nose again. "Or are you one of those wham-bam, thank you, ma'am guys like Mick Crowell?"

"Let's talk about it later, hon." He steered for the door with Cory wiggling to the beat of the music and bumping her hip against his for emphasis.

Outside, she smiled and waved to Shad who was talking to a group of bikers leaning against their Harleys. She gave the bikers a thumbs-up and they returned the gesture. Holt kept her tucked in the crook of his arm as they strolled down the street.

She breathed deeply of the night air. "I feel like I'm floating. Just like a cloud."

"I'm not surprised," he said dryly.

As Holt helped her upstairs, he was torn between wanting to laugh and itching to chew her out. He didn't know why this spitfire had taken hold of his heart, but she had. He'd almost broken his neck to get back to the Furnace. He didn't like the idea of her messing around on Sixth Street with another man. Hell, he didn't like the idea of her messing around anywhere with another man. Not with that Shadrach oddball or with the slick-looking comedian.

It wasn't that he was jealous. He'd never been particularly jealous of a woman before. He hadn't been jealous of Mary Ann, and they'd been engaged for six years. But Cory Bright did stir some strange new feelings in him. Sort of . . . possessive feelings. Protective feelings. As if he felt responsible for her. He almost laughed aloud at the thought. Cory would have a cat fit if he told her that. She'd made her independence damned clear.

Inside the apartment, Cory smiled brightly and once more tapped his nose with the flower. "Well, here we are again."

She looked so cute, he couldn't scold her. He smiled too.

"Are you going to kiss me this time," she asked, "or are you going to leave me puckered up and feeling silly?"

"My mama raised me to be a gentleman. I'd never take advantage of a lady who had a snootful."

"I do not have a snootful. I'm only a little tipsy."

He gave her a skeptical look. "How many of those rum bombs did you say you had?"

She held up five fingers. "Three." She cocked her head and squinted at him. "I wonder if you're really like Mick Crowell."

"His gut tightened. "Who's Mick Crowell?"

"Mr. Wham-bam, Thank You, Ma'am. Have you ever been married?"

"Nope."

"I have."

"Mick Crowell?"

"Heavens, no. I'd never marry a cretin like him. Donald was a poet."

"A poet? I didn't know anyone could make a living these days as a poet."

"He didn't make the living. I did. He took care of our apartment and wrote, and I was an account exec. It seemed like a fair division of labor. Donald was very gifted. He was sensitive and sweet and gentle."

Holt felt his gut tighten another notch. "And?"

She fluttered her hand. "He ran off with the Avon lady. Donald said I was too overpowering for him. Do you think I'm overpowering?"

"Hell, no. You're just right."

"Have you ever been engaged?"

"Yep. Once."

"Why didn't you get married?"

He shrugged. "I guess it wasn't in the cards. She married an elementary school principal."

"That's a coincidence. One of the men I was engaged to was an elementary school principal. He was a very nice man. He married a kindergarten teacher."

"*One* of the men? How many times have you been engaged?"

"Only twice, not counting Donald. They were both sensitive and sweet and gentle. But things just didn't work out between us. Things didn't work out with Woody either. And he was such a nice man. Every one of them had all the qualities I admire in men, but *pfffttt* and it fizzled. I can't for the life of me figure out where things went haywire. Do you think there's something wrong with me?"

The look in her eyes squeezed his heart like a fist. He gathered her in his arms and hugged her. "Hell, no. Not a damned thing I can see."

He patted her back while she nestled her head against his shoulder. The smell of her filled his nostrils. Even over the perfumed air of the apartment, he recognized her scent, vibrant and womanly and sexy as hell.

"There must be something wrong," she murmured. "Peter Fisher moved in with someone else a month before our wedding."

"The man was crazy."

"No," she sighed against his shirt. The warmth of her breath made him catch his. "He was gay."

"And you never caught on while you were engaged?"

"I simply thought he was shy and, you know, old-fashioned. I found it sweet. Are you old-fashioned, Holt?"

He snorted. "Not like that."

"I'm a strong woman. Do you think men are turned off by strong women?"

"Some men maybe. I've always preferred a filly with spirit over a docile mare."

"Are you comparing me with a horse?"

He laughed. "Bad analogy. I guess I've been spending too much time at the ranch."

"You have a ranch?"

"My brother and I have one. It's about an hour east of here."

"You have a brother?"

"Ummm." She stayed snuggled in his arms. It felt good. Damned good. "Two. One three years older, one a half a shake younger. No sisters."

"I have four brothers. All older. They're jerks."

He started to laugh, but the sound died in his throat when her hand moved from where it rested on his chest, sliding under his jean jacket and up to his shoulder. His muscles tensed.

"Your shoulders are very broad." Her hand returned to his chest and made circles across his pectorals. They started twitching like crazy. "And your chest is very muscular. Hard. I've never cared much for muscles, but yours are . . . nice," she purred.

She pushed away and looked up at him. Her long, silky hair framed her beautiful face like a honey-colored halo. The pupils of her eyes were large and black. Their blackness seared a hole in his resolve. He felt it disintegrating like burning cellophane.

"But," she said, "your lips look very soft."

His body heated and his blood surged. He ought to leave. He ought to go out that door right now. But his boots felt like they were dried in gumbo. She licked her lips and he groaned.

"Don't do this to me, Cory."

She smiled slightly, just enough that a dimple teased beside her mouth. "Do what?"

"If you keep this up, I'm going to kiss you."

"Why?"

"Because you turn me on like a house afire."

She lifted her face and challenged him with her eyes. Holt never could pass up a challenge.

Cory closed her eyes as his lips touched hers. They *were* soft, she thought. And sensual. And hungry. The tip of his tongue drew a slow trail across her open mouth, then nudged it wider. She obeyed. His tongue intruded boldly and captured hers. Her knees weakened.

He made a low, guttural sound and deepened the kiss with an energy that shot off rockets in her head. She moaned and clutched fistfuls of his shirt to stay on her feet. The power and urgency of his lips moving over hers, the feel of his solid body as he pulled her closer set her burning. She was melting inside. Aching, throbbing. She met his kiss, fire with fire.

His size, his strength, his raw virility enfolded her and made her feel deliciously feminine.

And vulnerable.

And powerless.

And frightened.

She stiffened. Her heart pounded faster. She whimpered and pushed against his chest with her fists.

Immediately, he released her and stepped back. His eyes were hooded and his mouth glistened with the wetness of their kiss. His chest rose and fell with deep breaths. "What's wrong, Cory? Did you get in over your head?"

"I—I don't know what you mean." She glanced away from those black eyes that seemed to read her mind.

He lifted her face and made her look at him. "I'm not one of those wimps of yours to be led around by the nose. I'm a man. Don't start it if you don't mean to finish it."

Anger came to her rescue. "I should have known that a chest-beating type like you would assume that a simple kiss was an invitation to bed. I suppose that if you'd raped me, you'd have said that you couldn't help yourself or that I'd asked for it."

"Dammit, woman, you can provoke me worse than the devil! We're a hell of a long way from the bedroom. I've never forced a woman in my life, and I have damned little patience with men who do. In fact, I think the gutless lizards who hurt women ought to be castrated and thrown under the jail for a hundred years."

She closed her eyes and took a deep breath. "I'm sorry. That was a lousy thing for me to say."

"Yes, it was. Apology accepted. I shouldn't have kissed you tonight. I knew you'd had too much to drink. I apologize."

"I'm stone sober now." She smiled. "Apology accepted."

He ruffled her hair and returned her smile. "I do mean to have you, Cory Bright. But I'm not just talking about making love with you."

She stood speechless, apprehensive—and a little excited, too, if she were truthful—as he picked up his hat, which had fallen to the floor. He set the Stetson on his head, gave it a tug, then turned and walked to the door.

He set the alarm and, with his hand on the knob, grinned back at her and winked. "Keep this locked. And don't open it to strangers."

Four

"You shot my car!" Cory leaned over to touch the three bullet holes piercing the trunk of her baby-blue BMW. "Would you look at this?" She turned back to glare at Holt. "Would you just look!"

Holt ambled over to the car parked inside the police pound. "Yep. It looks like I hit it all right." He opened the door and peered inside. "But you're lucky it's in good shape otherwise. It hasn't been stripped. I guess the guy was in too big a hurry."

"Why am I not consoled? Look at all that black gunk all over everything inside." Grimacing with disgust, she tore open a towelette she'd had in her purse and wiped fingerprint powder off the steering wheel. "Not only is my car a mess, but my face and name are plastered on the front page of the morning newspaper. To top it off, it was a lousy picture. I looked like a demented washerwoman."

Cory had been appalled to find the awful photo staring at her when she'd unfolded the paper that morning. With the story of the robberies and murders had been an account of the attempted holdup at the convenience store. Her name and address, as well as her ownership of Mignon's Sixth Scents, had been included in the article. The paper had related that she could identify the robber who escaped, and that the police planned to have her make a sketch of him.

"At least the reporter spelled your name right," Holt said, "and you got a plug for your business. Think of it as good advertising."

"Fine for you to say. That idiot didn't even get a clear picture of you. My mobcap and your hand blocked everything except your hat and your chin. And I noticed that they only referred to you as a local Texas Ranger."

He shrugged. "I like to keep a low profile. What happened to your belief in freedom of the press?"

Muttering under her breath, she thrust another towelette pack at Holt and went back to wiping. "I hope my insurance covers bullet holes."

"I'm sure it does. I know a good body shop where the owner owes me a favor. He should be able to have it out for you in a couple of days."

"And what am I going to do for a car in the meantime? I have a thousand things to do. I have a meeting with Mignon's attorney. I have to stop by the warehouse and the bank, and—"

"No problem. I'll take you."

"But—"

"You know, it's the damnedest thing. Today your eyes look green."

She fought to keep from laughing. "Of course. I'm wearing a green dress."

• • •

That afternoon, errands completed, Cory settled back in the passenger seat of the big silver Lincoln. Her car was in the shop, and the perfume formula book was in her lap. Holt had insisted on chauffeuring her, waiting patiently while she met with the attorney, and the employees at the warehouse. He had taken her to lunch at the Four Seasons before their final stop at the bank.

Although his was a formidable and commanding presence, he was a very nice man, she decided as she watched him drive. During their time together, he'd casually performed a dozen small courtesies, opening doors, checking her comfort. He was gentlemanly, almost to the point of courtliness, in a way that was rare these days. Although she'd dismissed such behavior in the past as silly, sexist, and old-fashioned, she was forced to admit that she almost preened in the glow of his masculine cosseting. She found, to her chagrin, that she liked the feeling.

And she like looking at him. She liked the way his dark hair curled just behind his ear; she liked the way his hat sat low on his forehead and the way he squinted, his thick, black eyelashes meeting, when he was concentrating. And the way his square chin jutted, shadowed by a dark beard that no amount of close shaving could erase. And the way his full lower lip curved . . . and felt when it touched hers.

Her fingers clenched the notebook and her eyes closed as she remembered the sensation of his mouth on hers. Warm, wet, hungry. Very hungry.

She licked her lips. Heat flashed through her and she squirmed.

Suddenly self-conscious, she opened her eyes and their gazes met. He was watching her, a faint smile playing around his mouth, a knowing look of shared memory flashing in his eyes. She quickly glanced away. He was *not* her type, she reminded herself. She'd had a bit too much to drink the night before and had been carried away by the moment. She didn't intend for it to happen again.

"I really appreciate your help," she said, trying to cover the awkwardness she felt, "but I feel guilty about taking you away from your work."

"My hours are often flexible, and I have lots of vacation time built up. I enjoy being with you. Besides," he said, winking at her, "I *did* shoot your car."

She laughed. "I'm sorry I said that. I know you had no choice. I hope they catch old Pig-face. It's a shame they didn't get any fingerprints from my car. I suppose he wasn't in so much of a hurry that he forgot to wipe away his prints."

"He must be a pro with a record."

Holt pulled into a parking space in front of the shop. Cory automatically reached for the door handle, but a subtle signal from him checked her action. He walked around to her side and helped her out, shielding her from traffic with his body. Such a small thing, but his simple gesture made her feel positively mushy inside.

"Would you like to see the shop?" she asked.

He nodded, and they went inside. Cory introduced Holt to Barbara and Kim, one of the students who worked the afternoon shift. She smiled when Kim looked him up and down and her eyes rolled appreciatively.

"By the way," Barbara said to Cory, "I found a letter addressed to you when I opened up this morning. It wasn't an ordinary posting, but it was dropped through the mail slot. I put it on your desk."

After a brief tour, Cory and Holt ended in the back workroom. She flourished her hand over the laboratory. "This is where the magic is performed. And this"—she held up the formula book—"has all the secret potions." She laughed. "If only Mr. Bourquine could see me now."

"Who is Mr. Bourquine?"

"My high school chemistry teacher. He said I was a menace with a Bunsen burner and a test tube. But Barbara insists that I must be the one to mix the special orders that have to be filled soon. With my luck and lack of expertise, the poor governor's wife will probably smell like a bordello."

Holt laughed. "I doubt that. Something tells me that you can do anything you set your mind to."

"Tell that to Mr. Bourquine," she said as she stepped into the office to put the book on the desk. An envelope with her name printed across the front lay on the blotter. She picked it up and opened it. "I'll have you know," she went on, "that once I burned—" Her words froze when she skimmed the note. Her hands went cold; shivers raced up her spine and tingled her scalp.

"What did you burn? Cory?" He came up beside her. "What's the matter, hon? You look like you just stuck your hand in a sack full of rattlesnakes."

Quickly, she stuffed the paper back in the envelope and laid it facedown on the desk. "It's nothing." She tried to keep her voice normal, but the words squeaked out. She cleared her throat. "An order for perfume." Stretching her lips across her teeth in an effort to smile, she said, "Thanks for all your help today. I really appreciate it."

He stepped back to lean against the doorjamb, looking amused. "Is that a hint for me to leave?"

She waved her hand toward the formula book. "I have hours of work to do figuring out how to mix perfume."

"Want me to stay and help? I was pretty good in chemistry."

"No, thank you." She twisted a fold of her skirt around her finger.

Furrowing his brow, he peered at her from under the brim of his hat. "Are you sure you're all right?"

"I'm sure. And I've kept you from your work long enough." Would he never leave so that she could have a nervous breakdown in peace?

He shrugged. "I took the whole day off."

"Then I know you must have a million things to do. I always have a long list of errands when I have a day off. I'll walk you to the door."

He seemed reluctant, and she held her breath. Finally, he walked over to her and lifted her chin with his index finger. "I get the message, sweetheart. How about dinner tonight?"

"Fine, fine." Anything to get him out of there. "But I have to be home early."

"I'll come by about seven." He gave her a soft kiss. "Don't forget the sketch."

Panic shot through her, and she stiffened. "What sketch?"

"The one of Pig-face the robber, remember? Lieutenant Morino said he'd drop by for it later this afternoon."

She closed her eyes and took a deep breath. "I remember."

Maybe she should tell Holt, she thought. No, the note said not to tell anybody. But—oh, hell's bells! She had to have time to think.

Holt gave her another quick kiss and left.

Cory sank down in the chair, plunked her elbows on the desk top, and buried her fingers in her hair. What was she going to do?

With shaking hands, she picked up the envelope again and took out the single sheet of paper with her picture from the *Austin Statesman's* front page taped to it. Her face was slashed with a red marker. Printed under it in bold letters was: KEEP YOUR MOUTH SHUT AND FORGET WHAT I LOOK LIKE OR YOUR DEAD. DON'T TELL NOBIDY ABOUT THIS. I'LL BE WACHIN.

"Dumb jerk can't even spell," she muttered.

As she stared at the words and the mutilated picture, her initial shock and fear subsided. She took several deep breaths and tried to control her emotional reactions, tried to be rational and objective. She doubted very seriously if the man was hanging around Sixth Street watching her. And how would he know if she'd made the sketch or not? Pig-face was bluffing, trying to scare her into keeping quiet. The police couldn't pick him up unless she made the sketch to identify him. The sooner he was arrested, the better. He was dangerous only as long as he was loose.

"Nice try, creep. I don't like being intimidated."

She clenched her teeth and grabbed a sheet of paper and a pencil.

After half an hour, she studied the drawing she'd made, then changed the shape of his eyebrows and altered his nose slightly. She studied it again and grinned. "Gotcha!"

In less than fifteen minutes, the short, gray-haired Lieutenant Morino arrived. Cory gave him the sketch and the note, explaining how Barbara had found the envelope.

"I don't think there's anything to worry about," Morino said. "I imagine he dropped this note and left town. I'm surprised he stayed around here this long. It's too hot for him on the streets. But to be on the safe side, you should be sure to keep your doors locked. And I wouldn't go out alone for a few days. We'll run a check on the description and the sketch. If he's got a record, we'll identify him soon and put out a pickup on him."

"What about King Kong? Do you have any information on him?"

The officer looked puzzled. "King Kong?"

"The other robber. The one who was shot. He wore a gorilla mask."

"He's in the hospital and recovering, but he's not talking. We've identified him. He has a previous arrest for armed robbery."

Barefoot, dressed in an old pair of shorts, and with her hair caught up in a ponytail, Cory stood at the work counter. The loose-leaf formula book lay open to the page headed by the name of the governor's wife. While she rolled up her shirt sleeves, she glanced at Barbara.

"Are you sure you don't want to do this?" Cory asked. "You're bound to be better at it than I am."

Barbara laughed. "Oh, no. Mignon was always very secretive about her blending process, and I respect her desire for confidentiality. But if I might suggest . . ."

"Suggest away. I don't know what in the dickens I'm doing."

"Mignon always wore rubber gloves and a lab coat. Most of the ingredients are quite concentrated and tend to cling to one's skin and clothes."

Cory rummaged through the drawers until she found a box of surgical gloves. "I'll have to skip the lab coat. Mignon is six inches shorter and two sizes smaller than I am." She snapped on a pair of gloves and held up her hands. "I feel like I'm about to perform brain surgery or some bizarre variety of safe sex."

Barbara giggled behind her hand. "Good luck. There's a new supply of crystal bottles in the third cabinet on the left. Rachel is here to help Kim with customers, and if you don't need anything else, I'm off for the day."

"Thanks for your help. Did you explain to Kim and Rachel that if anyone strange calls or comes by, I'm not in?"

"Yes, but I didn't go into any details. Do you think you're safe here? Perhaps you should spend the night with John and me or go to a hotel."

"I don't intend to be intimidated by some low-life

criminal. The doors have good locks, and I have the alarm system for both here and the apartment. I'll tell Shad to keep an eye out as well. I'll be fine, but thanks for your concern."

Barbara hesitated. "Are you quite sure you'll be safe?"

Cory nodded. "If you find me conked out in the morning, it will be from an overdose of"—she picked up a labeled bottle, sniffed its contents, and gave a cross-eyed grimace—"musk ambrette. What is this stuff anyway?"

"Musk ambrette is a fixative. This is a synthetic substitute for an ingredient extracted from an Asian male deer. Mignon preferred to avoid the use of animal products."

"I'd think the deer would be glad to be rid of it. It's vile smelling. Are you sure it goes in perfume? I wouldn't want it on my body."

"All the musks, both natural and synthetic, are both potent and essential. They're quite lovely after blending, but so penetrating as a concentrate, they can't be washed from polished steel."

Cory stoppered the bottle quickly and returned it to the shelf. "Hence the rubber gloves."

"Correct."

After Barbara left, Cory took a small beaker from the shelf. "Well, Mr. Bourquine, we're on. Let's see, three-fourths ounce Base Number Two."

She was pleased to discover that there were several large jugs of five different bases, preblended and suspended in denatured alcohol. Having them made her job much easier. It was simply a matter of adding a few drops of rose oil, a smidgen of jasmine, a squirt of vanilla, and a drop or two of this and that from five other bottles on the shelf.

"'Adder's fork and blind worm's sting, lizard's leg and howlet's wing . . .' *Heh-heh-heh,*" she cackled in her best witch imitation as she stirred the beaker's contents with a glass rod.

She sniffed the blend. Smelled pretty good. Reminded her a bit of lemon-scented dishwashing detergent, but without so much of a citrus kick. She funneled the contents into a crystal bottle and set it atop the order sheet at the end of the worktable.

Piece of cake, she thought. While she was on a roll, she picked up another special order, another beaker, and flipped through the book to Jessica Kaufmann's name. Base Number Four. When that lady's scent was done, she started another, then another.

"'Scale of dragon, tooth of wolf,'" she intoned, counting drops of exotic ingredients into the basic mixture. She wiggled her bottom as she stirred and recited other snippets she remembered from *Macbeth.* "'Double, double toil and trouble; Fire burn, and caldron bubble.' *Heh-heh-heh.*"

There was a pounding on the door. She shrieked and the beaker shot out of her hand and shattered at her feet. "Dammit!"

Olivia Lamb's perfume, liberally laced with ylang-ylang, patchouli, and heliotrope, soaked her clothes and ran down her legs to puddle between her toes.

The door flew open. "What the hell's going on in here?" a deep voice demanded.

Cory glanced over her shoulder to see Holt Berringer, clad in a sport coat and bearing a huge bouquet of yellow roses, striding toward her. She couldn't decide which was more overpowering—his scowl or the smell wafting up from her clothes and the floor.

"You startled me," she said, "and I dropped Mrs. Lamb's beaker."

"Don't move," he ordered, glaring at the pungent splashes and glass smithereens scattered over the floor. "Where are your shoes?"

"Upstairs."

"These are for you."

He handed her the big bundle of flowers—there must have been three dozen of them—then swung her up in his arms and stalked across the room. She clutched the roses in her rubber-gloved hands as he sat her down on a high counter and hung her feet in the stainless steel sink. He turned on the water and held his fingers under the faucet, testing the temperature.

"What in the world is this stuff? It smells like a cathouse in here." He squirted liquid soap on her legs and feet and worked up a lather.

"It *was* Olivia Lamb's special perfume blend. What are you doing here?"

"It's after seven o'clock. We have a dinner date."

"Seven? Already?"

"Yep."

"I'm not dressed."

He grinned. "I noticed."

Suddenly, she was aware of his strong hands massaging her toes. Her instep, her arch. Her heel, her ankle. Her calf. She closed her eyes and gave over to the delicious sensations and gentle ministrations of his hands. Her knee. Her inner thigh. His thumb circled, crept higher.

She grabbed his hand. "I don't think it splashed there."

His eyes sparkled with sensuality, and he gave her a slow, movie-star smile. "I was just being thorough."

She cocked an eyebrow.

He laughed.

When both feet and legs were washed, he said, "I think you're going to have to bury those clothes. Or maybe you can soak them in tomato juice. That's what we do when we tangle with a skunk."

He dried her with paper towels, swung her around, and stepped between her legs dangling from the counter.

"Thanks," she said. "And thanks for these." She brushed her face against the yellow buds. "They're lovely."

Cupping her face in his hands, he ran his thumbs along her jaw to her chin and back again. "You're more lovely."

She tried to say something, but the power of his gaze halted the words in her throat. His eyes scanned her face, their touch as intimate as any caress. Her skin flushed, then chilled, then flushed again. This was totally absurd, she told her pounding heart. But something about Holt Berringer—no, *everything* about Holt Berringer—pushed all her emotional buttons and had those emotions whizzing up and down like an express elevator.

His lips parted slowly and lowered to hers. A

thrill swept over her as she savored the warm taste of him. Although the kiss was gentle, a promise of wildness brewed beneath the surface calm. He nudged closer against the juncture of her thighs and thrust his tongue into her mouth.

Sighing, overcome with sensation, she clutched the bouquet in a death grip. The movement of his lips and his tongue intensified and sent her soaring. Her toes curled, and she crushed the roses tighter.

Pain shot through her finger, and she sucked in a startled yelp.

Holt pulled away, his expression troubled as his eyes searched his face. "Did I hurt you?"

"My finger. A thorn, I think."

"Oh, sweet," he crooned, taking the injured hand to examine it. "I'm sorry." With his tongue he bathed a drop of blood from her little finger, then kissed it.

She sat motionless, mesmerized by the movement of his tongue and his lips, wishing that they would touch a hundred other tingling places on her body. She shook herself from her musing and tried valiantly to remind herself that he was not the sort of man who appealed to her.

"It's not your fault," she said. "That is, it *is* your fault, but—Oh, hell's bells, I'd better go get dressed. If you don't mind waiting a few minutes, I'll clean the mess in here and change."

He shook his head. "You might cut yourself. I'll clean the mess in here. You go upstairs and dress."

Both of them acted reluctant to move. His eyes seemed to devour her as his thumb brushed the curve of her cheek. Then a puzzled look crept over his face. He leaned close and squinted.

"Why," he asked, "if you're wearing a purple shirt, are your eyes green?"

Relieved that the spell was broken, she giggled. "It must be the fumes." She scooted off the counter and hurried toward the door. "Give me fifteen minutes."

It was closer to twenty minutes later that Cory gave her hair a final swipe and tugged the hem of her powder-blue cotton sweater into place. She stuck her hands in her pockets and turned in front of the mirror, enjoying the feel of her full floral-printed skirt swirling around her legs.

When she walked into the living room, she was surprised to find Holt lounging in an easy chair, one booted ankle resting on the opposite knee. He rose as she entered.

"How did you get in here?" she asked.

"I came up the stairs from the shop. Kim showed me the way. You forgot to lock the door. That's not a good habit."

"Sorry. I was in a hurry. I'll lock it now."

He captured her in his arms as she passed. "I took care of it." He gave her a brief kiss, then drew back and smiled. His smile faded into a perplexed expression. Still holding her chin, he turned her face back and forth, studying her eyes.

Schooling herself to look as innocent as Mary's lamb, she asked, "Is something wrong?"

"Craziest damned thing I ever saw. Your eyes are baby-blue."

"I'm wearing a blue sweater."

He turned her face back and forth again. "You're wearing contact lenses.

"Yep."

"Are they tinted?"

"No, they're clear. Want me to take them out and show you?"

His eyes narrowed. "Do you have some tinted lenses?"

"Yep." She grinned. "Several pairs."

He laughed and touched his forehead to hers. "Thank the Lord. I thought I was going loco. You smell good—like yourself again."

"And you smell like Olivia Lamb. I forgot to tell you to put on rubber gloves. That stuff is potent. The synthetic musk fixative makes it linger, even after scrubbing. Take off your jacket and roll up your sleeves."

He cocked a brow. "Are you going to soak me in tomato juice?"

"No." She laughed. "Come with me." She led him into the bathroom and poured vinegar on his hands.

He rubbed his hands together, then sniffed them. "Works all right. I don't smell like a cathouse anymore. Now I smell like a pickle."

"Nag, nag, nag." She captured his wrist and drew a finger to her mouth, nibbling it playfully. "I may take a bite out of you. I'm starving."

"Help yourself."

His finger teased at the crease of her lips, gained entry, and trailed slowly along the edge of her bottom teeth. She bit down lightly, capturing it, and the tip of her tongue played over the pad of his finger. Then she looked up. His lips were parted, his nostrils flared. Desire, penetrating and palpable, smoldered in his eyes. The power behind his gaze was like a living thing, huge and pulsating and growing.

Her heart fluttered; her chest tightened. A deep ache throbbed inside her.

"You can have as much of me as you want," he said, his words a husky murmur, "anytime you want."

The throbbing ache intensified, lower. She shuddered, awed by the magnitude of the moment. An irresistible force, barely leashed, teetered on the edge of a downhill run. A whisper, a tiny movement could set it barreling toward her.

She pulled back.

Taking a deep breath, she pasted on her "perky" face. "Right now I'd sell my soul for a fat, juicy hamburger."

He smiled a slow, sexy smile that started with his heavy-lidded eyes and spread to the corners of his mouth. "You want it, you got it. I know just the place." He sniffed his hands. "And I'll blend in with the trimmings."

While he rinsed his hands, she hurried out of the bathroom. But on the trip to the front door, she felt as if she were walking on a huge bed of gelatin.

In the car, Holt's presence loomed like the shadow of a giant bird of prey. On one hand, she felt like a rabbit, frozen, trembling, waiting to be snatched up and carried off in the talons of an enormous eagle. She should be running for her life. Yet at the same time she felt a strange exhilaration, a compulsion, a fascination with the profound, elemental vitality that vibrated between them. It rumbled like an awakening volcano. The potency of his presence was as awesome as the raw power of Mt. Vesuvius.

Get real, she told herself. She was neither a timid rabbit nor a virgin about to be sacrificed to a pagan god. She was a strong, mature woman who controlled her own fate. Holt Berringer was an ordinary man.

Strike ordinary. He was extraordinary. Big and bold and incredibly sexy. She wondered what it would feel like to make love with him. Would he be gentle or a little rough? How would his mouth feel on her breasts?

She stopped twisting the fold of her skirt long enough to glance at him. He winked at her! She quickly looked away. Could he read her mind?

And why was her mind entertaining such ideas? The fumes from Olivia Lamb's perfume must have made her goofy. Or perhaps she was simply hungry.

They stopped at Hut's, a little joint a few blocks away. The café was a lively place with banners, old license plates, and celebrity memorabilia covering every available inch of wall space. Most of the items looked as if they were relics from the forties and fifties—and the café was the same vintage.

By the time they'd had two beers each and she'd had the most delicious bacon-cheeseburger she'd ever eaten—and he'd had two—plus fries and onion rings to die for, she was back in control of her emotions.

It had been hunger, she decided, that had made

her think and act crazy. Definitely hunger. Or the fumes. Or maybe a combination.

The phone was ringing as Holt unlocked the door for her. She ran to answer it.

"I meant what I said in the letter," a gravelly voice said. "You finger me and you're dead."

"Listen, *creep*, I've already fingered you! Your picture is spread all over the state by now. You'd better find a rock and crawl under it." She slammed the phone down.

"Who was that?" Holt's tone was sharp.

"That pig-faced robber! He had the nerve to threaten me again if I don't forget what he looks like."

Holt scowled. "Again? Has he contacted you before?"

Cory told him about the note.

He ground his teeth around a very explicit oath. "Pack a suitcase."

Her brows shot up. "I beg your pardon?"

"With that guy making threats, until he's caught, you're moving into my suite at the Driskill."

Her brows arched higher. "You're nuts. I most certainly am *not* moving into your hotel."

"Okay, I'll move in with you."

"You will not!"

"It's one or the other. Take your pick."

"Listen, Mr. High-and-Mighty Texas Ranger, nobody tells me what to do. Nobody."

Five

Cory stuck her nose in the air and flounced down the hall. "You can put your things in this room."

When Holt eyed the single bed with its fussy, flowered chintz canopy, she stifled an urge to snicker. To give him credit, he didn't say a word, even though there was considerably more of him than there was of the bed. She had its twin in her bedroom and, although it had been cozy for the petite Mignon, Cory would have been more comfortable with a larger place to sleep.

He hung his suit bag in the closet and started putting away items from another case. "This will be just fine," Holt said.

Liar, she thought with a smug grin. He was going to be miserable.

"If you don't mind, I'm going to use the bathroom first," she said. "Then I'm going to bed."

He left his unpacking and walked over to her. Very gently, he took her face in his big hands and lifted it until their eyes met. "Hon, I know you're aggravated with me, but I'm only doing this for your own good. You need a man here to protect you."

She jerked away, planted her hands on her hips, and thrust out her chin. She started counting silently, but her temper only rose with each number. "That's a hell of a thing to say! You sound exactly like my father. Men aren't the only creatures on this earth with sense. I can take care of myself, Holt Berringer, and don't you forget it!" She glared up at the six and a half foot man and poked his chest with her finger, accenting each word as she repeated, "Don't you forget it."

Whirling around, she stomped out the door and slammed it so hard, the pictures jiggled against the pink-flowered wallpaper. Holt tossed his Stetson on the dresser and ran his fingers through his hair. He'd torn it now. Cory was madder than a yellow jacket in a syrup bucket. He hated that because he was crazy about that little chameleon-eyed cyclone. She'd blasted into his heart like a Colt .45, and he was already thinking of her as his. Another door slammed in the apartment, and he winced. Yep, she was *some* peeved at him.

But he'd rather have her mad than dead. And she was in danger. No doubt about it. When he'd called the Austin PD to report the phone call, he'd learned that, thanks to Cory's drawing, old Pig-face had been identified. He was Warren "Skeeter" Sikes, an ex-con with a long sheet, who was not too swift and meaner than a wild boar in a ditch full of hounds. Sikes had done eight years hard time and had been released from Huntsville

Prison only two weeks before. And rumor had it that he didn't intend to go back. King Kong was his baby brother, Royce.

Cory could stew all she wanted to. He was staying. He'd called his captain and taken off the rest of the week. Until Sikes was caught, he was going to stick to her like sweet to sugar.

"I made coffee," Holt said when Cory appeared in the kitchen the next morning. He sat at the table reading the newspaper. "I couldn't find any bacon or eggs in the refrigerator or I would have fixed breakfast. We can walk over to the hotel after a while." His gaze traveled over her in a decidedly lascivious manner.

She tugged the lapels of her robe together and tightened the belt. "Thank you, but I don't eat breakfast."

She poured herself a mug of coffee, sat down, and blocked out his hulking presence with a section from the newspaper. Hadn't she told herself repeatedly that she shouldn't get mixed up with this Tarzan? she thought irritably. But had she listened? Oh, no. Her brains had taken a vacation and sublet her head to her glands. Now look at the mess she was in. She would simply pretend that he didn't exist.

"There's not much else in the refrigerator either," he said. "We'll need to go to the grocery store today."

Trying to make her tone as icy as possible, she said, "I'm sure that I don't care what you do,

Sergeant Berringer, but I'm not planning to go to the grocery store. I don't cook."

"Not at all?" He sounded incredulous.

"Not at all."

"What do you eat?"

"I have TV dinners or I go out."

"Okay, I'll cook when we don't go out."

She lowered the paper and glared over it. "And just how long do you intend to intrude in my life?"

He gave her a slow grin. "As long as it takes, sweetheart."

"Don't call me sweetheart," she snapped, jerking the paper up again.

"Testy this morning, aren't we?"

"I—I didn't sleep well. You snored so loudly that it sounded like a freight train inside the apartment."

It was a lie. He didn't snore. Or, at least she didn't hear him if he did. But she hadn't slept. She would have died before she admitted it, but Pig-face, or Warren Sikes, being on the loose bothered her.

Having Holt in the apartment bothered her too. Knowing he slept in the next room with only a thin wall between them had kept her tossing and turning most of the night. She couldn't blame her restlessness on fumes or hunger. Something about the man made her go all gushy inside. She kept imagining herself curled up beside him in the tiny bed, feeling safe and snug with his arms around her. The idea was preposterous. She had absolutely no intention of becoming emotionally involved with Mr. Macho. If, momentarily, her hormones had fogged her brain, his brutish attitude the night before should have been the antidote. Yet for some strange reason, the idea of being in his arms kept swirling in her head.

She had risen early from her tangled sheets and escaped to the bathroom. That was worse. The room was damp and warm from Holt's even earlier shower. His distinctive masculine scent hovered in the air. His razor lay on the sink; his red toothbrush hung intimately next to her blue one.

"Planning to buy a used car?" he asked.

"Pardon?"

"You've about read the ink off the want ads."

"I always read the classifieds. I find them fascinating." Not that there was a speck of truth in what she'd said. It had been the first section she grabbed.

He handed her another part of the paper. "You might find this more interesting."

Her drawing of Pig-face was on the front page beside a mug shot of Warren Sikes. "Hmmm," she said, sipping her coffee as she read. "My sketch was pretty good. And at least they only identified me as 'a witness' this time."

"They were a day late and a dollar short. Sikes already knows who you are." He pointed to another article. "Read this."

"About a fire at the hospital? It says that there were no injuries and the damage was minor."

He nodded. "But they're missing a patient. Royce Sikes, the one you call King Kong."

"You think Warren helped his brother escape?"

"I do. And anyone who'd set a diversionary fire in a hospital is crazy enough to do anything."

She shuddered. "Surely they wouldn't hang around town now."

"Might, might not. But that pair can't be counted on to be logical. From all accounts, the two of them put together don't have as much sense as a box of rocks. Pay attention to me when I say they're dangerous."

The phone rang and Cory started, sloshing coffee across the newspaper.

"I'll get it," Holt said. When he rose, she saw the gun clipped to the belt of his jeans and felt a margin of relief. He barked "hello" into the receiver twice, then hung up.

Her heart was beating ninety miles an hour, and her stomach felt as if it had dropped down an elevator shaft. "Nobody there?"

Holt shook his head.

He didn't have to say a word. They both suspected who'd called. She looked at the big man as he sat back down across from her and thanked her lucky stars for him.

She smiled. "Can you really cook?"

"You bet. All Rangers can cook. Sometimes you have to rustle up grub over a camp fire when you're in the saddle trailing a desperado."

She laughed. "When have you ever chased bandits on horseback?"

"Oh, if I remember correctly, the last time was when I was about twelve. And the bandits were imaginary. But my brother Ross and I did cook over a camp fire. As I recall, we had hot dogs and marshmallows. Boy, they were good." He grinned. "All this talk about food is making me hungry. Why don't you get dressed and come watch me eat."

She changed quickly into jeans and a T-shirt. After the door was locked, Holt laced her fingers into his and they walked to the Driskill Hotel for breakfast.

For the rest of the day, he barely let her out of his sight. He helped her blend special-order perfumes, escorted her across the street for lunch, and pushed the buggy down the aisles at the grocery store. Stetson pulled low over his forehead, and jean jacket collar flipped up, he looked totally out of place in the produce section—kind of cute and endearing, but out of place—yet he seemed to know what he was doing. The bill for the heaped cart was almost two hundred dollars, which he insisted on paying.

She eyed the mountain of sacks in the back seat of his car. "Are you sure you can cook?"

He winked. "Trust me."

As usual, he came through. The beef Stroganoff was delicious, the broccoli was perfectly steamed. The only flaw in the meal was the garlic bread. She'd fixed it while he sliced fresh peaches for dessert. The loaf was soggy on one end and dry on the other with enough garlic in between to clear the sinuses, but, bless him, he didn't so much as raise an eyebrow.

"I told you I couldn't cook," she offered as an apology. "I think I must have a mental block. In the Bright family, cooking was always considered 'women's work,'" she said with a touch of bitterness. "My mother discovered early that I am totally inept in the kitchen. I was assigned to table setting and dish washing while she prepared the meals and my father and brothers sat with their feet propped up watching television."

"My mother wouldn't have put up with that for a second. She's a war-horse. She insisted that my brothers and I learn how to do everything—cook, clean, and sew enough to replace a missing button. I never was much good at ironing shirts, though. I think Tessie, our maid, sneaked around and touched them up for me to keep me from being embarrassed. Now I send everything to the laundry."

She laughed. "I think I like your mother. I can't imagine any of my four brothers ironing a handkerchief, much less a shirt."

As they cleared the table, the phone rang. Automatically, Cory reached for it. Holt grabbed it first and gruffly said, "Hello." After a brief interrogation of the caller, he put his hand over the receiver and asked, "Do you know anyone named Howard Ellison?"

She frowned. "No."

After questioning the person further, he said to Cory, "He wants to talk to you about a job."

She took the call and spoke briefly with Mr. Ellison. By the time the conversation had ended, she was smiling.

"You look like you just won the lottery," Holt said. "Good news?"

"Howard Ellison is a headhunter from California. He heard from a friend of mine that I was free, and he thinks he knows several firms who might be interested." She grinned and punched the air. "Isn't that fantastic?"

"Sure." Holt picked up the silverware from the table.

"You don't sound too thrilled."

He shrugged. "I figured you were going to be around awhile."

"I never intended—"

The phone rang again. This time it was for Holt.

"Do you mind if I take this in your bedroom?" he asked.

"Take it here. I'll run downstairs and check on the shop before it closes."

"No!" He grabbed her before she moved. "You're not going anywhere without me."

"Not even downstairs?"

"Not even downstairs."

She heaved a theatrical sigh. "I'll be in my bedroom, *master*. Filing my nails."

A few minutes later, Holt rapped on the door, and she opened it.

"How would you like to go to San Antonio for a couple of days?" he asked. "I need to tend to some business there, and we can do some sightseeing."

"What kind of business?"

"Important business."

"That's no answer."

"It's better if you don't ask questions."

"But I can't just—"

His mouth shut off the words. His lips were oh, so soft; his tongue was oh, so insistent. She sighed as he teased her lips apart and delved into her acquiescence. Reason tumbled into oblivion and sensation took its place. She stood on tiptoe and lost herself in delicious abandon. He kissed better than any man she'd ever met. He made her melt like ice cream in August.

She never knew if the kiss was only to shut her up, but it was effective.

Cory stood on the balcony of her bedroom in their elegant suite overlooking San Antonio's riverwalk area. Leaning on the railing, she peered down at the sights below. There were several shops that she was dying to explore, and the boats navigating the meandering water looked like fun. Sounds of mingled conversations and laughter drifted up to her, along with a mélange of spicy aromas, baking bread, and sizzling meats. The scents reminded her stomach that it was lunchtime.

She brushed her hair and wandered into the living room to wait for Holt. A few minutes later, he came out of his bedroom. She did a classic double take.

The perennial cowboy hat was gone. His wavy hair was blown-dry within an inch of its life, and not a single hair so much as bent from its perfectly sculptured place. Handsome Italian shoes replaced the boots that she'd begun to think were permanently stapled to his feet. In between his hatless head and his bootless feet, he wore a gray silk suit, a dazzling white shirt, and a burgundy foulard tie—all well cut and obviously expensive. He was always a handsome devil, but this Holt Berringer could have held his own on Wall Street.

"Well, look at you," she said.

His hand went to the knot of his tie. A heavy gold Rolex watch and a diamond pinkie ring that looked like something from Liberace's estate sale flashed with the movement. She giggled. She was used to the watch, but a *pinkie* ring?

"Is something wrong?" he asked.

She looked down at her plaid shirt, khaki skirt, and sandals, then back at him. "We don't exactly match. Where did you have in mind for lunch—Maxim's?"

Fighting a smile, he cleared his throat. "I thought I'd take care of my business first, then we can go sightseeing. Why don't you order lunch from room service? I shouldn't be gone more than an hour or two."

Her disappointment must have shown, for he leaned over and gave her a soft kiss. "Sorry, kitten. I'll make it as quick as I can. Then we can see the Alamo, Sea World, and watch the sunset from the Tower of the Americas."

"I still don't understand why you won't tell me what kind of business you're here for. Is it some secret Ranger stuff?"

He looked pensive for a moment, then said, "My family has extensive real estate holdings around the state. Usually my older brother takes care of the family business, but once in a while Ross or I have to handle things. I have to meet with a group who wants to buy one of our buildings here."

"Well, why didn't you say so in the beginning?" She cocked her head, her brows drawing together. "Is your family *wealthy*?" She clapped her fingers over her mouth, horrified that she'd asked such a question. "I'm sorry. You don't have to answer that. It's none of my business."

He smiled. "Let's say we're very comfortable."

"Then why in the world are you a Texas Ranger?"

"Because I like it." Grinning, he tapped her nose with his forefinger. "Don't stick this pretty nose outside this room until I get back, hear?"

She didn't reply.

"Hear?"

"I hear. I hear."

When the door closed behind him, she made a face. "Order and demand. Order and demand."

Picking up a room-service menu, she made a half-hearted selection and, when it arrived, ate it with a similar degree of indifference. She tried watching TV but soon lost interest. Instead she wandered out on the balcony again. Holt had been gone for almost two hours, and she was growing restless. Across the river from the hotel was the cutest little boutique. A colorful assortment of items in the window beckoned her.

What could it hurt? Surely Sikes hadn't followed them to San Antonio.

She scribbled a note, grabbed her purse, and headed downstairs.

In her rush toward the hotel's front door, she almost collided with Holt and two men who were coming out of the bar.

He scowled.

Instead of cowing and turning tail as she was supposed to, she presented him her most dazzling, innocent smile. "Oh, hi there."

His scowl deepened. "What in the hell are you doing out of the room?"

Embarrassed, she glanced at the swarthy men with him. They looked like a pair of undertakers. Neither of them cracked even a tiny smile.

"I asked you a question," Holt said. "What in the hell are you doing out of the room?"

Fury flashed over her. "Listen to me, Ho—"

He grabbed her cheeks with his thumb and fingers and pushed them together until her lips poked out like a dying goldfish's. His eyes narrowed, and jaw muscles twitching, he stuck his face in hers. She could feel the anger pouring out of him. "When I tell you to do something, I mean for you to do it. Get your butt back up to the room. *Now.* Hear me?"

His tone was so menacing, his expression so deadly that her heart almost stopped. She didn't know this man. He'd gone crazy. Dr. Jekyll and Mr. Hyde. She'd almost fallen for a madman. Her eyes widened, and she nodded her head as best she could with his vise-like grip on her face.

One of the undertakers snickered. "Can't control your woman, Fields?"

"I can control her. Now, *git*," he said to Cory.

She got.

Blood pounding in her ears, her legs shaking, she ran to the elevator and punched the button several times before it opened. Thank heaven the cubicle was empty. She stabbed the number of the floor and slumped against the oak paneling, trying to calm her breathing before she hyperventilated. She couldn't remember ever being so scared in her life. Even her hair trembled.

When the elevator doors whooshed open, she bolted toward the room, unlocked it, and slammed the door shut behind her. Her first thought was to call the police. No, she couldn't do that. Holt *was* a lawman. And, oh Lord, he had a gun. She had to get out of there. Fast. She might be gutsy, but she was no fool. As big as he was and as angry as he was, Holt could make mincemeat out of her in nothing flat.

She threw her clothes in her bag and raced from the suite. After punching the button for the elevator, she suddenly stiffened. *Ohmylord.* What if he was on the elevator?

She sprinted for the stairs and made it down six flights in record time. Panting from the exertion, she eased the door open, poked her head out, and checked the lobby. All clear.

Fighting to control the hysterics threatening to overwhelm her, Cory walked briskly to the front desk.

"Where may I rent a car, please?" she asked the clerk.

As she listened to directions to the rental office, a big hand clamped her shoulder.

She froze.

"Where do you think you're going?" Holt asked gruffly as he turned her to face him.

"Tokyo, Brazil, Zambia. Somewhere, anywhere away from you. Let me go or I'll scream."

"Sweetheart, let me explain—"

Cory saw red with jagged black bolts and bubbling orange spots. She slapped his hand away. "Sweetheart? *Sweetheart?*" she shrieked.

He touched her cheek gently. "Honey, listen to—"

"Don't you touch me, you cretin! I'm out of here." She turned back to the wide-eyed clerk who'd gone pale as a Kabuki actor. "Call security."

Holt shoved a leather-encased badge under the

poor man's nose. "Texas Rangers," he said in a low voice. "Git."

The clerk got.

"Babe, if you'll listen to me for a minute—"

"Drop dead. I'm not going to stay around for your abuse." She picked up her bag, thrust her chin in the air, and started for the front door.

The next thing she knew, her feet had left the floor and she was dangling over Holt's broad shoulder.

She screamed bloody murder.

Six

With Cory yelling and pounding on his back, Holt kicked their suite door closed and strode to her bedroom, ignoring her colorful castigation and vehement insults to his parentage. The moment he tossed her onto the soft bed, she bounded up and stuck her face as close to his as she could get it, given the difference in their heights. He had to admire her grit; she didn't seem at all intimidated by him. Eyes blazing blue fire and her face red as a beet, she stuck her fists on her hips and shot him a look designed to peel his hide.

She tried to stalk past, but he blocked her path.

"Out of my way, you—you overgrown, grunting Neanderthal! I'm leaving!"

"If you'll just let me explain—"

"Explain? What's to *explain*? You're nothing but a bully, and I will not tolerate remaining in the same room with such an abusive, sorry excuse for a man for one single solitary second. Some women may be turned on by such caveman tactics, but I'll have you know, buster, *I'm* not one of them. I don't care if you're a Texas Ranger or the President of the United States! Nobody, *nobody* treats me like a sack of garbage."

Holt felt like a dirty dog. "Sweetheart, just listen for—"

"I wouldn't listen to anything you said if you offered me a billion dollars. You are the scrapings of the earth." She tried to shove past, but he pinned her in his arms.

"Honey—"

"Don't you 'honey' me, you north end of a south-bound mule!" She struggled in his arms like a sackful of wildcats. "Let me go!"

"Sugar, please give me—"

"I wouldn't give you a bucket of water if your hair were on fire." She stomped on his foot and beat on his chest, but he held her firm.

"Dammit, Cory, I was undercover and you almost blew it. I had to say what I did to shut you up."

Her struggles ceased. She pulled back and, eyes narrowed, looked up at him. "Undercover?"

He nodded.

"You aren't here for a real estate deal?"

He shook his head.

"Then you lied to me?"

The censure in her voice made him feel lower than a snake's belly. "Yep. Had to. I told you to stay put until I came back."

She stiffened. "Yes, you *told* me. I don't take orders from any man without reasons, and I don't like being lied to. If you'd explained things in the first place instead of ordering and demanding, I would have understood and this whole nasty mess could have been avoided."

"I'm not used to having to account to anybody."

"I noticed. *I'm* not used to being manhandled."

"Cory, most of my work is confidential. You're going to have to accept that. And I could get my tail in a crack for telling you as much as I have. I hated to be rough with you, but, babe, if those two thugs had gotten any inkling that I'm a Ranger, months of work would be down the tubes, and I'd be planted under the bitterweeds in a cow pasture somewhere."

"You mean they would have *killed* you?"

He nodded. "Deader than a doornail. That pair runs with some bad *hombres*."

She sucked in a gasp and her eyes glazed with tears. "Oh, Holt, I'm so sorry. I didn't know."

Hugging her close, he rubbed his cheek against her sweet-smelling hair. "I know you didn't, kitten. And I hated having to lie to you, but I could see you weren't going to be satisfied until I gave you some sort of explanation. You hit too close to the truth when you suspected that I had some sort of secret Ranger business."

"Then your family doesn't have property in San Antonio?"

He laughed. "That part was true enough, but my older brother does take care of family business. Anytime I have to sign anything, Paul sends it by Federal Express."

She snuggled in his arms and laid her cheek on his chest. Her hand smoothed the lapel of his coat. He was content, for the moment, just to hold her close and feel her body next to his. Her bones felt as delicate and fragile as a dove's.

"Holt?"

"Hmmm?"

"I won't tell anyone about your being undercover."

"I know you won't, love." He kissed the top of her head. She nuzzled closer and sighed.

"And if I run into you anywhere again, I'll pretend I don't know you unless you speak first."

"I don't think we'll have a problem. I don't do this often." Eyes closed, he continued to hold her, treasuring her soft warmth.

"Holt?"

"Hmmm?"

"I won't let those men hurt you."

Tenderness swelled his chest, and he smiled and squeezed her. If he hadn't realized before that he loved her, those simple words convinced him. He almost voiced his feelings, but he didn't figure Cory was quite ready to deal with them. Instead, he said, "Thank you, my fierce little guardian angel." He couldn't keep the grin from his words.

"I'm not kidding," she said seriously.

"I know you're not, kitten." He almost laughed at the thought of Cory spitting fire and wading into the Garza brothers. They'd probably never know what hit them.

Her hand slipped under his coat to stroke his chest. It seemed to sear through the thin cotton of his shirt. His belly contracted and his muscles tensed. His hands slid to her buttocks to knead their softness and pull her against his growing hardness.

"Holt?"

"Hmmm?"

"I think we'd better go see the Alamo."

They did indeed visit the Alamo. And Sea World. And the Tower of the Americas. With his arms around her waist and her head leaned back against his shoulder, they stood atop the tall structure and watched the sun trail its fiery orange over the horizon.

"I do love sunsets," Cory murmured as the tip disappeared, leaving behind a gold-touched pink-and-purple glow to stain the clouds.

His lips brushed her temple. "Soon I'm going to show you that special one I promised."

"You don't have to see those men again?"

"Not for a while."

After dinner, they strolled hand in hand along the riverwalk and had dessert at a sidewalk café. They didn't talk much. They only savored each other's nearness, silently sharing the sights and sounds of the city's heartbeat and the rippling, meandering water.

Later, in the elevator of their hotel, a chic blonde gave Holt an appreciative once-over, and Cory felt her hackles rise. She linked his arm possessively, sidled closer to him, and glared at the blonde. He patted Cory's hand and winked at her, oblivious to the elevator car's other passenger.

Cory's behavior surprised and confused her. Why did she feel possessive of Holt? She'd reminded herself a million times that he wasn't her type, and she had no intention of becoming emotionally involved with him.

But she *was* becoming emotionally involved. Somehow, when she wasn't looking, Holt had snuck into her heart.

Fleeting echoes of her father's and brothers' snickering catcalls chased through her head, and she clenched her teeth. Holt was exactly the kind of man they would approve of—a man's man. She could almost hear her father saying, "See, sister, I told you all you needed was the right man to tend to you."

Slipping her arm from his, she clasped her fingers together and stared straight ahead. She'd simply have to become uninvolved. She had bigger fish to fry. Everything she'd ever dreamed of was just around the corner, waiting for her in California. She planned to make it big, on her own. She wasn't going to allow herself to get tangled up with a black-eyed hunk of brawn and blow it now.

When they were inside the parlor of their suite, Holt reached for her. She neatly sidestepped and pasted a bright smile on her face.

"I had a very nice time tonight," she said. "Thank you for the evening."

He grinned meaningfully. "The night's not over yet." He reached for her again.

She sidestepped again and put the couch between them.

He frowned. "Cory, what's the matter with you?"

Her eyes widened. "Why, whatever do you mean?"

"You're jumping around like a cricket on a hot skillet. Are you still mad about this afternoon?"

"No, I'm not mad. I'm very tired." She faked a yawn. "I'm going to bed now. Good night."

He smiled. "Don't I even get a kiss?"

"No."

"Mind telling me why not?"

"Because my daddy would approve of you, and kissing you right now would be the dumbest thing I ever did."

He looked perplexed. "Mind running that by me again?"

"I'm going to California, Holt Berringer. And don't you forget it!" She stalked from the room and slammed the door.

Holt stared at Cory's door for a moment, frowned, and shook his head. What had put a burr under her blanket all of a sudden? She'd been as cuddly as a new puppy since their fracas that afternoon, and he'd thought things were going great between them. Surely he hadn't completely misjudged her growing feelings for him.

Her daddy? California? Why would kissing him be dumb? It didn't seem dumb to him. In fact, he'd had a little more in mind than kissing. Hell, he'd had a lot more in mind. He ran his fingers through his hair and mulled over her flip-flop in attitude. He could always blame it on PMS, but somehow that didn't wash.

Trying to make sense of the situation, he examined this piece of information and that, like putting together a jigsaw puzzle of Cory Bright. As the light began to dawn, a grin spread across his face. No, he hadn't misread her feelings. As a criminal investigator, he was a pretty good judge of human nature. For some crazy reason, she was running scared. Which meant she cared more than she'd ever admit.

He walked over to her door and tapped softly. "Cory?"

"Yes?" came the muffled reply.

"It won't work, honey. It's gonna be you and me."

Silence.

Hands in his pockets and grinning from ear to ear, Holt ambled toward his room, whistling. He'd spent a lot of time on stakeouts in the last few years. He'd learned to be a patient man.

By the weekend, Cory was about to go up the wall. Since he'd moved in, Holt hadn't let her out of his sight, and she was beginning to think they were going to be permanently joined at the hip. And the hip wasn't exactly where her fantasies wished they were joined.

There. She'd admitted it.

Being around him twenty-four hours a day swamped her with sexual frustration. Worse than frustration. Obsession better described her state. For as much as she hated to concede it, Holt Berringer was the sexiest thing in pants, and one of his smoldering looks could turn her into a mindless puddle and send her nerve endings thrumming like a flamenco guitar.

It hadn't helped to discover that he'd had a king-size bed delivered to her apartment while they were in San Antonio. The thing almost filled the small bedroom she'd assigned to him—and added another dimension to her recalcitrant imagination. With merely a flick of his lashes, a touch, or a smile, he could turn her inside out. If he'd been an obnoxious slob, tuning him out would have been easy. But he wasn't. In fact, he was a perfect gentleman. He was calm and amiable while she flitted around like a butterfly on a tether string—with Holt holding the string.

If this togetherness went on much longer, she was going to attack him. Only that morning she'd stumbled into the bathroom, still half-asleep from a restless night, to find him fresh from his shower and naked as a jaybird. She should have slammed the door and beat a quick retreat. But did she? Of course not. She'd stayed, glued to the spot and gaping like a ninny.

And he hadn't even had the decency to cover up. He'd simply stood there in all his glory and winked at her. Winked at her!

He'd given her one of those lopsided grins and asked, "See anything that particularly interests you?"

She'd dragged her gaze to his face and stuck her nose in the air. "You don't have anything I haven't seen before," she'd retorted, and flounced back to her room.

She'd lied.

He was in a class by himself. The man was gorgeous.

Their encounter had left her more anxious than ever. She'd thought about it all day long. And imagined that lovely, muscled body next to hers on his big bed.

As they sat in the living room on Saturday night after dinner, each supposedly engrossed in books they'd bought earlier that day, her gaze traveled over the length of him. His black boots sat beside his chair and his sock-clad feet rested on an ottoman. Remembering the hard thighs that his soft denim jeans covered, the broad shoulders and rippled chest his white western-style shirt hid, she went warm all over and her bare toes curled against the rug.

Holt glanced up from the Louis L'Amour novel he was reading and caught her staring at him. He smiled—an I-know-exactly-what-you're-thinking smile—and her gaze quickly returned to the thick saga in her lap. When she glanced up again, he was staring at her legs. She wiggled and tugged at her shorts. Their gazes met, and this time she didn't look away. Black eyes captivated her, taunted her, stroked her.

Desire hung in the air between them like a dense tangle of raw electrical wires hissing and sparking in a windstorm. All her senses swelled and ripened into a bittersweet yearning that robbed her of breath and reason.

For long moments, she was helpless in the onslaught. Muffled sounds of music and Saturday night revelry from the Sixth Street crowd sifted through the thick brick walls of the apartment, lending a background of bacchanalian enticement.

Holt's eyes focused on her lips. Her mouth went slack. His gaze swept over her breasts; they swelled and her nipples hardened beneath the pink T-shirt. His eyes met hers once again, a faint, sensual smile curving his mouth, brows raised in silent question. The beat of distant basses reverberated beneath her feet and quickened her longing, like jungle drums in a primitive fertility rite.

She closed her eyes and inhaled a deep breath.

"Cory?"

She opened her eyes.

"I want you."

"I figured as much."

His low, sexy chuckle rippled over her like an aphrodisiac. "Bright lady."

"How about a walk instead?"

He shook his head.

"Could I interest you in some hot chocolate?"

He shook his head.

"A cold shower?"

"Nope." He smiled. "I've had more than my share in the past few days. They're vastly overrated." He stood and, without taking his eyes off her, slipped gun and belt from his waistband.

Her gaze darted from his face to the gun that he laid on the table and back again. "What are you doing?"

He grinned. "Taking off my gun. I told you that I don't wear it *everywhere*." He walked over to her and pulled her to her feet. "I want you, Cory. And unless I'm seriously mistaken, the feeling is mutual. Am I wrong?"

"Why don't we go to the Old Pecan Street Café for some dessert? I'm starving for a slice of pecan pie. With a giant scoop of ice cream on top. Doesn't that sound yummy? Afterward, we could drop in and see Shad and Marcia at the Fiery Furnace. We haven't seen them in a couple of days. Better yet, I've been wanting to catch Sid's act at the comedy club on the corner. It's still early and—"

"Kitten," he said, silencing her by pressing two fingers to her mouth, "stop running." His eyes were lit with a combination of laughter and desire as his arms encircled her waist. "Tell me what you really want."

"You're not buying pecan pie?"

"Not for a minute."

With him so close, her senses raced into overdrive. The masculine smell of him intoxicated her; the heat from his body radiated through her. Her hands lifted to his chest, and she felt the powerful thudding of his heart beneath the soft cotton her fingers stroked. A patch of dark curls showed at the opening of his shirt. The patch mesmerized her, tantalized her. She popped the shirt's snaps until they were undone to his waist, then threaded her fingers through the black, downy hair on his muscular chest. The tempo of his heart increased, and she smiled.

She kissed the hollow of his throat and delved into the indentation with her tongue. His hands slid to her bottom and lifted her from the floor until they were face-to-face.

"Tell me, Cory."

Her legs locked around his waist. "You," she whispered against his lips. "Lord, help me, I want you."

His mouth covered hers with a hunger that sapped her soul. He alternately kissed her and whispered love words as he strode toward his bedroom.

With her legs still clamped around his waist, he sat on the bed. "I want to see you," he said, pulling her shirt over her head. "And I want to taste every bit of you." He unhooked her bra and flung it aside. His eyes scanned her bare flesh. "Beautiful," he murmured as he brushed his lips across a breast. "More beautiful than I imagined."

His tongue trailed a slow, wet circle around the peak of her left breast, and her back arched at the delicious sensation. His lips closed around the nipple and pulled gently. She moaned. As he laved his way down her sternum and back up to her other aching breast, she leaned back against his arms and lost herself in the erotic veneration of his mouth and tongue and hoarse words of praise for her body.

"All," he whispered against her abdomen. "I want to see all of you."

He set her on her feet and peeled off shorts and panties in one quick motion. Holding her at arm's length, he swept his gaze over her. He reached out to run his fingers over a curve here, a contour there. "Oh, babe." He groaned.

Rather than feeling self-conscious, she felt deliciously feminine. And proud. Basking in the tribute he paid and heady with power, she smiled. "See anything that particularly interests you?"

He grinned lopsidedly. "Yes, ma'am. Everything interests me, from here"—he lifted a strand of hair on the top of her head—"to here." He touched her toes. "And all that's in between." His hands slowly slid up the curve of her legs from ankle to thigh. "Especially here. And here."

When her belly contracted with his seductive caresses, he chuckled. "I want them all. Over and over." He stood, stripped off his shirt, and hurled it toward the corner.

Her breasts rose and fell with her rapid breaths as she reached for the front of his jeans, her fingers trembling. After a pop of the snap and a rasp of his zipper, she slid her hands down his hips, shoving fabric toward the floor as she reveled in the feel of his tense musculature. She rubbed her cheek against the dark hair on his chest and touched the tip of her tongue to his nipple. Her actions wrung a guttural sound from deep in his throat, and his fingers tightened around her forearms.

Between the two of them, his remaining clothes were impatiently dispensed until he stood before her, his big, corded body magnificently aroused. "Look what you've done to me," he said.

"Are you complaining?" she teased, stroking him.

His hand closed over hers. "Hell, no, but since I met you, it's become a permanent condition."

Excited by the notion, she laughed seductively and brushed her breasts against his chest. Grabbing her buttocks, he hoisted her against him, grinding her pelvis to his and hungrily reaching for her lips. Her laughter turned to a whimpering moan, and her fingers dug into his broad back as fire shot through her. She was a mass of writhing nerve endings, and every fiber in her body throbbed with hot eagerness. With frenzied movements, she strained toward the source of her need.

"Easy, easy, babe. We've got all the time in the world."

"Speak for yourself, Ranger. I want you *now*."

"Where do you want me, love?"

"Inside me. Deep inside me."

He raised her higher, then lowered her slowly

onto his waiting tumescence. The sweet fullness sucked a sharp breath from her, and her heels dug into his back as her head fell backward. With his tongue, he licked a wet path up the front of her throat to her chin. She gave a little cry and moved against him with mounting excitement.

"Oh . . . babe." His words were a deep groan. "I'm on fire for you." He laid their joined bodies on the bed and covered her face with kisses. "Tell me how you want it."

"Hot and hard," she demanded.

He met her demands with wild thrusting and unbearable ferocity. Her body growing damp and slick with effort, she matched his potency with a fierce taking and an unleashed rhythm that sent them spiraling into a beauteously, wondrously feral passion. Higher and higher they urged and pressed and pleaded in wordless cries. She drew in a sudden breath, spasmed, and shattered into a world lit by a million blazing stars. He tensed, shuddered, called out her name.

For long moments they lay there, warm naked flesh against flesh, stunned by the power of their lovemaking, basking in the afterglow of ecstasy.

Holt rolled aside and held her in his arms. When he spoke, his voice was husky with emotion. "Lord, how I cherish you."

Cory's heart stumbled at his words. The emotion of the moment, she rationalized, and pushed his declaration into a back corner of her mind. Her fingers tangled in the thick, damp hair on his chest. "You are, without a doubt," she said, "the most excitingly virile man I have ever encountered."

"I am?" She could hear the smug grin in his voice.

"You are. Sergeant, you're dynamite. Is that part of Ranger training?"

He chuckled. "I reckon it just comes naturally. With the right lady." He kissed her forehead. "And you're the right lady for me. I'm never going to let you go."

With his words, a sudden disquiet ruptured her euphoria.

"Holt?"

"Hmmm?"

"You do understand that anything between us is only temporary, don't you? When Howard Ellison called yesterday, he said that two or three agencies in California sounded eager to talk to me. If they come through with firm offers, I'll be going to L.A. in a couple of weeks for interviews. If one of the agencies makes the right deal, I'll be gone."

"We'll see."

"There is no 'we'll see.' I plan to move where the action is hot."

His fingers stroked up her thigh to the juncture of her legs. "The action is pretty hot right here."

She grabbed his hand. "I'm talking about *advertising.*"

"I don't think you need to advertise, babe. I'll keep you plenty busy." He nuzzled her neck and nipped at her ear.

"Holt, dammit, I'm serious. I'm going to California."

"What about Sixth Scents? You seem to be enjoying the business."

She chewed her lip. "It's been fun—temporarily.

But if I decide not to sell, I'll hire someone as general manager. In any event, *I'm moving to California.*"

"What about us?"

She huffed an exaggerated sigh. "That's what I've been trying to get through your thick head. There is no 'us.' You're not even my type."

"And what is your type?"

"Oh, someone who is gentle, sensitive, romantic, interested in the arts. You and I are totally mis—"

He cut off her argument with a kiss that almost sent her through the roof.

Seven

On Sunday afternoon, Cory and Holt were about to go out when his pager beeped.

"Sorry, kitten, but I'd better call in."

"I know the routine," she said. "You want me to wait here or in my bedroom?"

"I'll use the bedroom phone." He dropped a kiss on her sweetly pouting lips. "I won't be but a minute."

Holt closed the door and called headquarters. After a few minutes' conversation with his captain, he said, "Okay, I'll be in tomorrow, but I'd like to be able to spend nights here until he's apprehended." The captain made a laughing remark, and Holt added, "Sure, but you know how nervous women are about these things."

After he'd hung up, he sat on the bed with his elbows on his knees and his fingers laced together, thinking. The news was both good and bad. He debated about whether or not to tell Cory what he'd learned. He didn't figure that she would be nearly as nervous about the situation as he'd let on to his superior. His and Cory's relationship was at a critical spot, and he had a hunch that if she insisted he move back to the hotel, he'd lose ground with her. His strategy for winning her over was all mapped out, and having to leave now would put a crimp in his plans.

On the other hand, if he didn't tell her, and she got wind of it some other way, there'd be hell to pay. He took off his hat, ran his fingers through his hair, then resettled the Stetson low on his brow. He'd tell her . . . most of it.

Cory glanced up from a magazine and smiled as he entered the living room. She looked like an angel sitting there in a ruffly white sundress with her honey-colored hair forming a soft halo around her face and shoulders. Lord, he was crazy about her. No way was she getting away from him.

"That's a terrible scowl you're wearing, cowboy. Problems?"

"Not exactly." He forced a smile. "Royce Sikes was picked up in El Paso. Seems his shoulder wound got infected and he was running a fever, so his brother took him to a clinic for treatment. The doctor got suspicious and called the police."

"That's fantastic news! What about old Pig-face Warren? Did they get him too?"

"No, he got away. But we can rest easier knowing he's nearly six hundred miles away from here. Probably slipped over into Mexico. But it would be smart," he rushed on to say, "if we kept our guard up. You never know what he might do. I think, if you use good judgment, you'll be safe enough during the day while I'm working, but I'll continue to stay here nights until he's caught."

She cocked her head and studied him for a moment. "Sounds like a good idea."

He let out the breath he didn't know he'd been holding and grinned. "Ready?"

She nodded. "Where are we going?"

He tweaked her nose. "I told you, it's a surprise."

They locked up and went downstairs. Holt felt only a little guilty for not telling her the rest of it: The last time Warren Sikes was seen, he'd lit out toward Juárez with a bad bullet hole in his leg. There wasn't the chance of a snowball in hell that Sikes would show up in Austin. He'd be caught at the border and land in an El Paso jail. But Holt had to buy some time to show Cory how gentle, sensitive, romantic, and interested in the arts he really was.

They spent the afternoon at Laguna Gloria Art Museum, first holding hands and strolling the rock-paved paths through the grounds, a naturally landscaped area set on a craggy piece of peninsula that jutted into Lake Austin. Figuring that Cory would enjoy the charm of the scenery, he led her along a terraced walkway thick with oak, palm, and pecan trees that formed a shady canopy to the lagoon.

"It's beautiful," she said. "And cool."

"It's always cool here, even in the summer. The museum holds a big art festival every year with about two hundred exhibitors. It's coming up in a month. I think you'll enjoy it."

"I'll probably be in Los Angeles a month from now."

He clenched his teeth to keep from saying, "The hell you will!" Instead, he made a noncommittal sound and steered her toward the Mediterranean-style villa that housed a collection of twentieth century art.

When one of the female employees greeted him with fluttery deference, Cory raised an eyebrow. "Texas Rangers certainly get a lot of respect," she whispered.

"I doubt that she knows I'm a Ranger. I'm a patron of the museum," he said, fighting to keep the smugness from his voice.

"Oh, really?" She looked thoughtful.

He silently blessed his mother, who had always insisted her boys contribute to the arts. Writing checks every year to local museums and art scholarship funds had become a habit. He blessed Eleanor Berringer again when he was able to make reasonably intelligent comments on some of the paintings and sculpture displayed.

Later that afternoon, the sun hung low over Town Lake when Holt filled the bottom of a rented canoe with pillows and helped Cory in. He arranged the cushions so that she could sit stretched out in the hull and lean back against the seat.

"Wouldn't you rather I face the front and help paddle?" she asked.

"I'll handle the paddling. I'd rather be able to see your pretty face." He kissed her briefly, then set a pink egg carton and a small transistor radio in the boat and shoved off.

"Are you going to tell me what's in the egg carton now?" she asked.

"Later. Just relax and enjoy yourself."

"I'm very curious."

He smiled. "You know what happened to the cat."

Still puzzled, she reached for the pink container. He gently swatted her hand and ruffled her hair. She laughed and leaned back. He'd been very secretive about it. After they'd visited the museum, he'd stopped by the mall and insisted she browse through a boutique instead of coming with him. Fifteen minutes later, he'd returned with the mysterious pink box under his arm. She was dying to know what was inside the carton labeled only "Lamme's." All that he would tell her was that it was a rare Austin delicacy.

He tuned the radio to a classical station and turned it low. An enigmatic smile on his lips, he dipped the oar into the blue-green water with slow, even strokes, propelling them along the course that meandered through town and divided it north and south before it narrowed to become the Colorado River once again.

A faint breeze rippled the sun-washed surface of the narrow lake, and only the soft strains of music, faint sounds of laughing children playing in the park, and the rhythmic dip of the paddle breached the quiet of the tributary's verdant banks.

Cory let her fingers trail through the cool water and watched Holt maneuver the craft. The muscles of his arms bulged as he pulled against the water, and she remembered the wonder of the flesh now hidden by shirt and jean vest. The tall, brawny man with a silver star and a gun on his belt should have looked incongruous in the gentle, romantic setting, but somehow he didn't. He seemed very . . . sweet. Endearing. She smiled when a yellow butterfly landed on the brim of his hat, fanned its wings twice, then flitted away.

"Enjoying yourself?" he asked.

"Very much. It's lovely here."

Switching the paddle to the other side, he brought the canoe close to a low spot on the shore where a willow dipped its delicate branches over the water, and let the craft drift among the curtain of feathery limbs. Downstream, in a green-shaded alcove, three graceful white swans, undisturbed by human intrusion, glided along the dappled water.

"This is a perfect place to watch the sunset," he said.

The canoe rocked as he rose to tie it on to the tree. Cory grabbed the sides. "Careful. I wouldn't want to end up in the lake."

He chuckled. "Trust me. I was an Eagle Scout. These things aren't as easy to tip over as you might think." He tossed his hat aside and, after retrieving the pink carton, stretched out beside her on the pillows.

"Now will you tell me what's in the egg crate?" she asked.

"Close your eyes." When she did, he said, "Now open your mouth. Wider. Take a bite."

Her teeth slid through a luscious, rich confection. Creamy milk chocolate and fresh, ripe strawberry. The delicious contrast of velvety sweetness and juicy tartness melded into ambrosia against her tongue. "Mmmm," she said, opening her eyes.

"Mmmmmm. That's wonderful. I've never tasted anything so heavenly. I feel totally decadent."

"Good." He grinned and fed her another bite of the huge chocolate-covered strawberry. "I thought you might like some. These are only available twice a year. People line up for blocks to buy them."

Her eyes widened. "Then how did you get them so quickly? You were only gone for a few minutes."

He shrugged. "I paid a kid from the hotel to stand in line for me. He was almost to the front when I got there." He fed her another bite of the plump delicacy, then licked a drop of juice that trickled down her chin.

They sat among the billowing drapery of willow branches, laughing as they fed each other strawberries, and watched the gold-shot rays recede from the lake's surface. With the canoe cradling them in the gently swaying water, they commemorated the end of the day, sharing the moment as the sun painted the sky with its final glory and slipped beyond the horizon.

Only four strawberries were left. Holt picked up one from its nest in the carton and held it to Cory's lips. He brushed the sweet chocolate along them, but when she opened her mouth for the morsel, he withdrew it and licked her lips with his tongue.

"Your lips are sweeter than any strawberry," he murmured, then claimed a hungry kiss.

She tasted the mingled flavors of candy and fruit on his tongue as it delved into her mouth to tangle with hers. He smelled of sunshine and chocolate. His lips, warm and moist, sent a thrill scampering over her body.

His fingers flicked open the buttons of her sundress, and he nuzzled his face in the cleft of her bosom. His breath warmed her skin, and his nearness heated her blood. Her breasts ached for his touch. She threaded her fingers through his thick hair and pulled his face closer to assuage the ache. He groaned and his mouth slipped lower to nip at the sensitive peaks straining against the lace of her bra.

Stirred by the sensation, she arched toward him, and her legs moved restlessly as she tugged at his hips. He shifted his position and rolled his massive frame to cover her. The canoe rocked and bobbed with the movement, and from the corner of her eye, she saw his Stetson sliding toward the water.

She jerked up. "Your hat!"

They both made a grab for it. The canoe dipped and listed with their precariously shifted weight. Cory shrieked and flailed her arms for balance, but the boat tipped and spilled them into the lake.

Cory came up sputtering and laughing.

Holt came up sputtering and cursing. "Are you all right?"

"I'm fine." She held his soggy Stetson in the air. "I got your hat."

"Forget the damned hat!" He lifted her into his arms and waded out of the waist-high water, scowling and grumbling as he sloshed to shore in his wet boots. "So much for our romantic interlude." Disgust dripped from his voice like the water from their sodden clothes.

She kissed his damp cheek, sleeked back the black curls plastered to his brow, and stuck his hat on his head. "I think it's very romantic. I've never been rescued from a lake before."

"I'll bet no damned fool has ever dumped you overboard either."

She laughed and, throwing her arms around his neck, kissed his cheek again. "No, but it makes an interesting story."

His scowl deepened. "I'd just as soon nobody ever heard about it. If my brother, Ross, gets wind of it, he'll never quit hoorahing me."

Boots squishing with every step, he climbed the grassy bank and set her down. Brushing her hair back from her face, he squeezed water from it. He pulled the bodice of her sundress together, and his big fingers struggled to refasten the tiny buttons into the wet fabric. His expression of self-disgust grew as he gathered a bunch of her skirt, wrung it out, and flapped it, trying to dry the hopelessly soaked thin cotton. Her heart almost melted with his tender, awkward ministrations.

"Babe, I'm so sorry," he said, shaking his head.

"Hey, it's not your fault. We both made a dive for the hat. You got as wet as I did, and we'll both dry." She looked down at her bare feet. Giggling, she wiggled her toes. "We saved your hat, but I seemed to have lost my sandals."

"Damn! I'll see if I can find them."

He turned and started to slosh back into the water, but she stopped him. "Forget the shoes. I can get another pair. Did you lose anything? What about your gun? Your wallet?"

Slinging back his sodden vest, he patted his holster and its weapon, felt his pockets. "Nothing's missing." He looked her over and shook his head again. "I'll take the boat back and bring the car closer."

"I'll go with you."

For the first time since their misadventure, he grinned. "Honey, I think you'd better stay here. Wet, your dress is almost transparent. While I think you look damned sexy, that kid at the boat stall would have a heart attack."

She looked down at the white eyelet plastered to her legs. "I think you're right."

"I know I'm right. Even if he is barely old enough to grown peach fuzz on his cheeks, I don't want any other guy ogling you."

"Possessive, are we?"

"Damned right."

He gave her a hearty smacking kiss and slogged out to the canoe, turned it over, and grabbed the paddle that, thankfully, had wedged against a tree root. After he climbed in, he waved and told her he'd hurry. In his powerful hands, the paddle cut the water with quick, deep strokes that sent the boat slicing over the lake's surface. Fascinated by the beauty of him, she sat on a large rock and watched him, his broad back straight and his face carved into a grim stoicism that made his Cherokee heritage more apparent, until he rounded a bend out of sight.

What was it about Holt Berringer that fascinated and excited her so? She reaffirmed that he was nothing like the ideal man she had fantasized. On the one hand he infuriated her, yet on the other, he could make her sigh like a teenager over a rock star. She had to admit that while machismo radiated from him like gamma rays, there was more to him than swagger. He had substance. And he was the kind of lover that every woman dreamed of—considerate, bone-meltingly sensual, and very, very thorough.

Something else peeked out from the tough Ranger persona now and then. She smiled as she watched a pink egg carton ride a gentle swell and float toward the bank. He had a romantic streak tucked in the heart beneath his hairy chest. If she weren't careful, she could fall in love with the big lug.

And that would never do. She was moving to California, come hell or high water, dammit.

She hoisted her skirt and waded out to retrieve the pink carton that bobbled on the surface. Three big chocolate-dipped strawberries still sat in their compartments. She sighed, walked downstream to where the swans sat floating in the fading light, and tossed them one by one into the water.

The graceful white waterfowl ignored her proffered treat and swam away.

"Dumb birds," she called after them. "You don't know a good thing when you see it." They didn't even look back.

"Cory!"

"I'm here." She headed back to where Holt waited.

"We need to get you home and out of those wet clothes before you catch cold."

She smiled at his concern. Even in the gathering twilight, the temperature was still in the seventies. "What about you?" she asked as she picked her way over the grassy bank. "Won't you catch cold?"

"I'm tough."

"So am I." She stepped on a sharp rock and let out a yelp.

Holt strode toward her and swung her into his arms. "Naw," he said. "You're a tenderfoot."

Groaning exaggeratedly at his pun, she buried her face in the hollow of his shoulder and laughed.

"Did the boy at the boat rental place comment on your wet clothes?" she asked.

"Nope. I tipped him an extra ten soggy bucks and flashed my gun."

"You *didn't*!"

He laughed. "No, I didn't."

"Is your gun ruined?"

He shook his head. "I can take it apart and clean it. The stuff in my billfold is what's a mess. Will you iron my money?"

She grinned. "I don't iron, cook, or do windows. But I have other redeeming qualities."

He tapped her nose and winked. "I won't argue with that."

They drove to the Driskill Hotel, and Holt had the young man on valet duty drop them off in front of Sixth Scents before parking the Lincoln in the garage.

Once upstairs, they stripped in the bathroom and stepped into the shower together. Holt quickly scrubbed himself, then insisted on shampooing her hair and soaping her body. Halfway through the process, his soaping changed into more of an erotic rite than an effort to cleanse her.

With the fine spray pelting their bodies, she leaned back against him as he lifted her breasts with his forearm and rubbed the bar over their swells and peaks. He lathered his hands and circled them over her belly, kissing the cap of her shoulder and the nape of her neck as his fingers slid lower. And lower.

"Holt," she squealed, laughing. "You've already washed there. Twice."

"The third time is the charm."

As he continued his slow caresses of her body, she writhed against him, reveling in his hardness at her back, savoring the wondrous touch of intimate fingers and buffeting water. Heat rose inside her like the steam from the shower. She reached behind her, grasped his hips, and rubbed her bottom against him, purring like a cat being stroked.

"Feel good?" His tongue circled her ear.

"Mmmm. Too good."

"Can't be too good."

His teeth nipped at her neck, his hand stroked her breasts, and his fingers continued their magical rhythm. She moaned as she soaked up the swelling sensation like an insatiable sponge, until she reached a sudden, cascading release.

Knees weak, she lay back against him and savored the glow washing over her.

"Good?" he asked.

"Mmmm. Better than strawberries. But my legs are useless."

He chuckled and lifted her from the shower.

Two days later, Cory sat in the perfume lab, sniffing this vial and that before adding a drop to the glass beaker she held. She stirred the contents and sniffed again. Almost.

She added another drop of extract and swished the rod through the mixture. She passed the container under her nose for a whiff. Perfect.

There was a knock on the door, and Barbara stuck her head in. "Someone to see you. A Mr. Bonnell from New York. Shall I show him in?"

"In a minute. Come smell this and see what you think." Cory touched a drop to her forearm and fanned it to dry before she held it to Barbara's nose.

"Quite lovely. Something new?"

Cory nodded. "I've been experimenting. Tell me what it reminds you of."

Barbara closed her eyes and sniffed again. "It's fresh and quite tantalizing. I'm reminded of spring breezes, cascading water perhaps, strawberries and . . . a hint of something sweetly elusive and a bit sinful, like—" She frowned as if struggling to identify the scent.

"Milk chocolate?" Cory prompted.

"Exactly."

Cory laughed. "I did it!"

Barbara joined in her laughter. "You certainly did. I'm sure the new fragrance will be a great success with our customers. Especially the chocoholics like me. What will you name it?"

"I haven't decided yet. Finding a new fragrance name is difficult. All the good ones are already taken. I suppose for now it's Bright Number One." She poured the beaker's contents into a crystal bottle and snapped off her gloves. "What does Mr. Bonnell want, a special blend for his wife?"

Handing her a business card, the shop manager

smiled. "I suspect that he wants the formula book."

Cory read the gold-embossed name of a prestigious perfume company below the name of David Bonnell. She raked the edge of the card against her palm several times and took a deep breath.

"Show him in, please."

Eight

"So, have you decided to sell?" Holt asked.

Cory wiggled her toes in the new sandals he'd bought for her and leaned her head against the window of the silver Lincoln. "I don't know. Dave made the offer very appealing. He's a charming man."

Holt snorted. "That anemic-looking pansy from New York? Charming?"

"David Bonnell is *not* an anemic-looking pansy," she retorted with more vehemence than the situation called for. "He's . . . cosmopolitan . . . sensitive. And extremely knowledgeable about fragrances." She crossed her arms and huffed. "Oh, what's the use? I wouldn't expect *you* to understand."

His hands tightened their grip on the steering wheel and his eyes narrowed. Cory could almost see steam hiss from his ears. She didn't understand why she sometimes took such perverse pleasure in baiting him. Perhaps it was some deep need to defend herself from his blatant masculine appeal.

"I'm knowledgeable enough about fragrances," he said through clenched teeth, "to recognize a pile of fresh cow patties when they're waved under my nose. He's a pantywaist pain in the caboose. For two days I haven't been able to step for him in the way, fluttering around, kissing your hand, sucking up to you. I'm glad he's on his way back where he belongs."

Cory didn't comment. She felt like a hypocrite defending Dave. As much as she hated to concede the point—and she'd die before she'd admit it to Holt—David Bonnell had been a pain in the caboose. And compared to Holt, an anemic-looking pansy. A few weeks ago, she wouldn't have thought so. She would have been charmed by his urbane bearing, his European-style dress, his savoir faire. But she'd found his manner, which she once would have labeled as sensitive, irritatingly vapid.

"Our opinions of Dave aside," she said, "his company made a lucrative offer. I'm going to give it serious consideration."

"You've been having a high-heeled time mixing perfumes and messing around Sixth Street. I was kind of hoping you might change your mind and decide to stay in Austin."

"Nope." Determined to avoid further discussion of the issue, she promptly changed the subject to the wildflowers along the winding highway toward Lake Travis. "And the hills are so lush and green. They remind me of great heaps of giant broccoli bundles."

He chuckled. "The hills are covered with oak

trees. I'd never thought of it, but I guess that from a distance they do look kind of like big bunches of broccoli." He grinned at her. "But I'm not sure that's a very poetic description."

She made a face. "I'm not a very poetic person. I suppose that's why I admire people who are."

"Hell, I'm poetic. How about this: There once was a gal from Sioux City, whose figure was rounded so pretty. She jiggled and turned, and all the men burned, to reach out and pinch her—"

"Holt Berringer!" she shouted over the bawdy finish. She tried to keep a straight face, but an unladylike snort of laughter burst from her. "That's not what I meant by poetry."

"It rhymes, doesn't it? Want to hear another one?"

She rolled her eyes. "Give me a break."

Gravel crunched under the tires as they pulled up to a weathered wood cantina. "Here we are, kitten. The Oasis. It's billed as the sunset capital of the world."

Cory looked at the rather plain structure and raised her eyebrows. "Of the world?"

"That's what they say." He leaned across the seat and kissed her. "And the nachos and margaritas aren't bad either."

As they entered the cantina, filled with hot, smoky scents of sizzling peppered meat and pungent Mexican spices, Holt took her hand and led her through the crowded building to the back. From that vantage point, the view was incredible. They were atop a high hill that sloped down to the rock-carved banks of the huge lake. The outdoor part of the cantina, sculpted into the limestone cliff like a giant tree house, hung four or five hundred feet above the water.

People, laughing and talking, gathered on several levels that formed a warren of two dozen or more wooden decks jutting out from the hillside among the spreading oaks that clung to the rocky face. Striped umbrellas added gay color to the naturally weathered platforms.

Holt and Cory walked up and down and around a series of steps and passageways until Holt found a spot shaded by an ancient live oak and a yellow and white umbrella on the patio table.

"Perfect," he declared. He dragged his deck chair close to hers, so that when he tipped back, his arm rested along the top of her chair. His thumb stroked her shoulder and toyed with the thin strap of her camisole. "You like it here?"

She looked out over water glistening under the blinding, brilliant blaze of the setting sun. The liquid gold surface shimmered like fine champagne, and the sails of boats drifting across the lamé lake seemed swelled with gossamer light.

"Oh, Holt, it's spectacular."

A crooked grin teased at his lips. "I thought you might like it."

They ordered margaritas and nachos from a young blonde waitress, then settled back to enjoy the sun's fiery display. As it became a huge orange globe pulsating above the hills, Cory rested her head in the crook of Holt's shoulder and allowed the serenity of the early evening to wash over her.

She almost regretted the intrusion when the waitress returned with their order balanced on a tray. The perky young blonde set a platter of spicy nachos on the table, then reached for one of the frosty margaritas that were served in paper cups. Whether the waitress was too occupied ogling Holt to pay proper attention to her task, or whether the cup was slippery, Cory would never know. But the slushy, salt-ringed drink dropped.

The waitress squealed, Holt made a valiant grab, and Cory tried to scoot out of the line of fire. The tequila mixture landed with a splashing plop on her foot. She leaned over slowly and peered at the icy mush dribbling down her instep. The lime slice jeered up at her from its precarious balance on her big toe.

"Damn!" Holt spat.

"Oh, I'm so sorry," the waitress exclaimed. "Let me get you another drink."

Thoroughly disgusted with the mess, Cory wiggled her toe and the lime slid off. Holt scowled at the waitress as she scurried away, then grabbed a handful of napkins and tried to blot up the melting concoction as it trickled between Cory's toes and leaked into the sole of her sandal.

She stripped off her shoe and with the aid of the napkins, Holt's handkerchief, and four tissues offered from gawking patrons at nearby tables, they mopped most of the sticky liquid from her foot and dried her new sandal.

"Babe, I can't tell you how sorry I am. I wanted this to be special. Seems like I'm always having to wash your feet after some mess I've caused, and our sunsets seem to be snake-bit." Distress furrowed his brow as he knelt before her, giving her foot a last pat with the tail of his shirt. "You want to go?"

His vulnerable, hangdog expression touched her heart. She plucked off his hat and kissed his forehead. "Certainly not. I'm here to watch a sunset."

And watch it they did. The sight was magnificent. Heads together and sipping margaritas, they followed the sun's exit as it sank lower and lower. When the last sliver of the fiery ball slipped behind the hills, a loud bell clanged and the entire gallery rose and applauded nature's showy exhibition. Holt and Cory rose with them, laughing and clapping.

"Did you like that, kitten?"

"Oh, I *loved* it!" She threw her arms around him and hugged him. "Thank you."

His dark eyes shone like the gold-washed water, and he rubbed his nose across hers. "I'll have to find some other special spots for sunset watching."

They had another drink while the crowd thinned, then made their way back up through the main lodge. When Cory kept limping oddly, Holt stopped and looked down at her feet.

"Is something wrong?" he asked.

She giggled. "Even though it's dry, my foot is gummy. My toes keep sticking to the sole of my sandal and slurping every time I take a step."

He scowled. "Damn."

"Don't get in such an uproar. It will come off with a little soap and water. I'll stop by the ladies' room and wash."

"I have a better idea," he said, a lascivious glint in his eyes. "Why don't we go home and scrub it good in the shower?"

Remembering the things that invariably happened when they shared a bath, she wrapped her arms around his and gave him a flirtatious, knowing look. "You're becoming quite attached to my shower, aren't you?"

"Babe, I may have it bronzed."

On Sunday afternoon, Holt was nervous as he and Cory drove along Mo-Pac, the expressway that followed the Missouri-Pacific railroad tracks on the west side of Austin. He'd done everything he could think of to prove that he was gentle, sensitive, romantic, and interested in the arts.

He'd tried his damnedest not to cuss too much. He'd sent her flowers every day; paid a mariachi band two hundred bucks to serenade her under her window the other night; and clomped through every museum, art gallery, and exhibit in town. Hell, he'd even bought a new tux and reserved tickets for the opera. He'd about worn himself to a nub trying to keep her happy in bed—not that he was complaining. The lovemaking between them was mind-blowing, and being around her kept him hornier than he'd ever been in his life. But *still* she hadn't wavered in her determination to move to California.

He never had thought much of California before. Now he was beginning to hate the place.

That afternoon's plan was a new twist. He'd appeal to her nesting instincts *and* her artistic flair. He exited the freeway and headed toward a residential area on Lake Austin.

"Are you sure you don't mind doing this?" he asked.

"Heavens, no," she said. "I want to see your house, and, anyway, I love decorating. Give me a paint chart and a bundle of fabric swatches, and I'm as happy as a tick on a hound."

He chuckled. "You're beginning to talk like me."

"I grew up in Goat Hill, Arkansas, remember? They have a few colorful phrases there too."

He wound through the shady streets south of the Westwood Country Club, then pulled into his driveway. It was good to see the place again, finally completely renovated. They got out and strolled up the winding rock walk to the front door of the Mexican brick and natural cedar split-level.

"Oh, Holt, it's lovely. I'll bet you were devastated about the fire damage. Were you at home when it happened?"

"No, I was out of town. The neighbors called the fire department. I came home to a holy mess. The smoke and water damage was pretty bad. Most of the inside had to be gutted and rebuilt."

Leaves rustled in the big oak tree beside the entry, and Cory glanced up. "Look, a squirrel. Isn't he adorable?"

Holt grunted. "I'm not too high on squirrels right now. One of those little critters chewing on wires in the attic was probably what started the fire."

He unlocked the double doors and ushered her inside to the fresh smell of new wood and plaster. Hearing Cory's quick intake of breath, he grinned like a fox in a henhouse. She liked it. Chalk up one for his side.

"Your home is beautiful, really beautiful." She walked down the steps from the flagstone entryway and across the empty, concrete-floored living area to the broad expanse of glass across the back.

He followed her. His arms circled her waist, and he pulled her back against his chest and imagined her living there, in his house, with him. Although the swimming pool, built of natural stone and carved into a terrace on the bluff, was empty now, he imagined her standing nude at the edge of the waterfall, laughing before she dived in. He imagined her sitting with him on the patio, sipping their coffee and enjoying the early morning view of the lake.

Lord, how he loved her. His soul ached to tell her that she'd become his world, that without her his life would be empty and bleak. He wanted to beg her to stay in Austin, marry him, have his babies, hold hands with him, and watch sunsets as they grew old together.

Instead he waved his hand over the empty room and said, "As you can see, there's a lot to be done yet. Paint, wallpaper, carpet, furniture, the works."

"Wasn't anything saved?"

"I managed to salvage most of my clothes and a few other things. What's left of the furniture is stored in a warehouse. Babe, if you don't want to mess with this, I guess I can always hire a decorator."

She turned in his arms. "Don't you dare! Show me the rest. I'm itching to get my hands on this place."

"My hands are itching for something else." His

palms slid down her back to cup her bottom. He wiggled his eyebrows. "The bedrooms are upstairs."

"But there aren't any beds, are there?"

"We can improvise."

She laughed. "You are the randiest man I've ever encountered. Which way is the kitchen?"

"That way." He tilted his head toward double doors near the huge fieldstone fireplace. "I've never made love in the kitchen before. Sounds kind of kinky, but I'm game."

She giggled. "That's not what I had in mind. I was thinking of color schemes."

"I was too. I like those little blue panties you're wearing. They match your eyes."

"Wrong. Look again."

"Oops. They're green today."

"Right. Let's look at the kitchen." She grabbed his hand and charged toward the end of the room.

A smug smile stole over his face as he let her drag him from the room. His plan was working like a charm. With any luck, it would take a month or six weeks to fix up the house. At least that's what the expensive decorator he'd hired had told him. Which reminded him, he'd have to call and cancel her services. She might squawk a little, but he'd pay her a hefty bonus. Keeping Cory around was worth any amount of money.

Cory ran her fingers over the hand-painted Italian tiles set into the wall behind the kitchen counter. "I'm glad these weren't damaged. They're exquisite."

"This part of the house wasn't hurt too badly. The floors were flooded and the wallpaper was ruined. Think we should paint the cabinets dark brown?"

She looked horrified. "Certainly not! The room should be light and airy—a rich cream maybe, with touches of turquoise and brick-red to coordinate with the tiles."

"I concede to your superior taste." He lifted her onto the counter, touched his lips to hers, then ran his tongue over their lush fullness. "And you do taste superior."

Their mouths merged with breath-stealing enthusiasm. He'd meant only to share a kiss, but, as always, when he felt her eager response, a kiss was not enough. He wanted to inhale her, devour her, drink her up, join their bodies, and bury himself in her sweet heat.

Oh, kitten, I love you so, his mind whispered. *Don't leave me. Please don't ever leave me.*

"I want you so much. Let me give you the world," he murmured aloud.

Tuesday morning, as soon as Holt kissed her good-bye and left for headquarters, Cory ran down the interior stairs to the lab and filled the most pressing orders. Her task was completed long before time for the shop to open. She had the rest of the day to spend on Holt's house.

Back in her apartment, she gathered paint color chips, three books of wallpaper samples she and Marcia had found the afternoon before, and several fabric swatches she was considering. She located the inventory she and Holt had made of his things in the warehouse, then crammed everything in a large satchel, along with her notebook and tape measure.

She lugged her materials down the block to the parking garage across from the Driskill Hotel. Storing her car in the garage was a hassle, but Holt had convinced her that leaving it parked on the street was asking for trouble.

She didn't need any more trouble. Though she was likely to get some that night. Holt would probably have a fit about her going to the house by herself, but he had work to do and Marcia had classes that morning. Besides, they had seen neither hide nor hair of Warren Sikes since he'd been reported heading toward Mexico. Even if he had been around, he wasn't likely to attack her in broad daylight. Anyway, he was probably holed up in Juárez, drinking tequila.

When her things were stowed in the back seat, she tooled down the ramp and waved to the attendant as she left the garage. After a brief stop to pick up carpet samples, she drove to Holt's house.

A few minutes later, she stood in the living area with swatches, books, and samples scattered around her. She could almost visualize the room. A moss-green carpet stretched out in her imagination. The paneling was stained a rich walnut, books filled the shelves, and the furniture was an eclectic blend of traditional and contemporary. There would be plush couches in a fabric that picked up the green of the carpet, and big easy chairs in soft leather. The glow of brass lamps lit the room and a fire crackled in the fireplace. She could almost see herself with Holt, sitting curled up on the couch, watching the flames.

She shook her head. No. She wouldn't be there. Someone else would be curled up beside him. A hollow ache gnawed at her stomach. She ignored it and escaped to the kitchen with color chips and wallpaper books.

Her gaze flew straight to a spot on the counter. A flush spread over her as she remembered what had happened there Sunday afternoon. Would he do the same things with someone else once she was gone? A fierce possessiveness stirred inside her. She tamped it down and decided to deal with the upstairs before she made any decisions about the kitchen.

Sitting on the floor of the master bedroom, she pictured a huge bed covered with a bold paisley comforter and great mounds of pillows. Holt's laughter and whispered endearments echoed in her head. Wouldn't it be lovely to wake up there every morning in his arms and feel his breath warm against her cheek?

She blew out a puff of air. She couldn't be both there and in Los Angeles. And she *was* going to Los Angeles. When the right job opened up, she would be off like a shot. She was good at what she did, dammit. She knew the business and her plans were made. For a few years, she'd work her butt off for a top-notch agency, then she would gather a team of talented comers and form her own agency. It would be a success. A big success. With an enviable client list.

How she would crow. Some Christmas, when her family was gathered for the holiday, she'd drive up to her parents' house in Goat Hill—in a red Ferrari or something that would look ostentatious beside the pickup trucks and Chevrolet sedans they drove— and rub her daddy's and her brothers' noses in it. She would flash her diamond rings, casually toss aside her full-length sable, and name-drop like crazy. Perhaps her fantasy sounded small-minded, but she didn't care. All her life she'd been determined to prove to them her value as an independent woman, and, by gum, she meant to do it.

Besides, she and Holt were only temporary lovers. True, the loving was wonderful, but he hadn't given any indication that his feelings went deeper. While he had uttered some potent phrases in bed, that was only pillow talk. Oh, he'd made lots of noises about wanting her to stay in Austin, but it wasn't as if he'd seriously declared his undying love and proposed marriage.

Cory shook her head. How had her thoughts strayed to marriage? She might be a little bit in love with Holt, but once she left Austin, it would pass. Certainly, she would never consider marrying him.

Even if he asked.

She spent the next several hours walking through the house, holding colors and papers up to the walls and making notes. By midafternoon, she'd completed her preliminary plans, and her rumbling stomach reminded her that she'd skipped lunch.

After she locked up, she drove back to Sixth Street. Her empty stomach grumbled even louder as she smelled food from Scandals, the corner bar and grill of the Driskill. Following her nose, she walked inside the eatery and took a window table.

"What can I get you?" a waitress asked.

"I'm starving," Cory said. "What do you recommend?"

Taking the waitress's suggestion, she ordered a cheeseburger, french fries, and iced tea. While she waited, she toyed with a book of matches and glanced around the room.

Too late for most lunch patrons and too early for happy hour, the place was almost deserted. A young couple sat in the corner gazing into each other's eyes; three men in suits gestured in earnest conversation at a table; at the bar, a big cowboy nursed a beer and laughed with a full-bosomed redhead in a low-cut top, who brushed her breasts against his arm and ran her toes up and down his leg.

Cory's gaze slid idly to the bartender who was polishing brandy snifters, then she started and her eyes swung back to the cowboy. She frowned. His back was to her so she couldn't see his face, but . . .

No, it couldn't be.

He'd worn a gray western suit that morning, not jeans and a vest. Yet from the rear, the cowboy in the black hat with a jaunty feather looked remarkably like Holt.

As if he felt his neck prickle from her stare, the man glanced over his shoulder. Her heart almost stopped.

It *was* Holt. And he hadn't even acknowledged her! He'd swung back around and laughed at something the blowsy hussy said.

Blood-red sparks erupted in front of her eyes as fury exploded inside her. Who in the hell did he think he was? She'd been working like an army mule all day to make his house livable. She'd fretted and stewed and gone without lunch, while *he*, the conniving jerk, played footsie with a bimbo in a bar. And he'd had the gall to ignore her! She was halfway out of her seat to beat him over the head with a wallpaper book, when reason shoved her back down in the chair.

He'd changed clothes. He'd ignored her. Could he, perhaps, be undercover again? She dared not endanger him if he were. She glanced over at the men in suits. Now that she thought about it, they looked shifty-eyed and mean. Maybe they were drug dealers and Holt was tailing them.

But who was the redhead? She looked like a hooker. Was she really a policewoman in disguise? An informant?

The floozy leaned over, whispered something to Holt, then stuck her tongue in his ear.

Cory's eyes popped wide as she sucked in a loud breath. She averted her gaze, grabbed the tea glass the waitress plunked before her, and swallowed down half the contents.

She tried not to look, she really tried. But her gaze swung back to them like a tongue to a sore tooth. *She was nibbling his earlobe and her hand was on his thigh. Very high on his thigh.* Cory gulped the rest of her tea.

The cheeseburger was delivered. She took a bite, but it felt like a volleyball in her throat. She dragged a french fry through a blob of catsup and tried to eat it, but it lodged in her esophagus and it took three swallows to get it down.

She told herself that she should just pay her

check and leave, but she was glued to the chair in morbid fascination. When his fingers walked down the tart's backbone and patted her ample fanny, Cory wanted to rip a leg off the table and beat him over the head with it.

"Want some more tea?" the waitress asked.

"Leave the pitcher."

She gulped another glass down and watched the spectacle at the bar, trying to control her temper, trying to tell herself there was some rational explanation for his behavior. It didn't help. She seethed. She fumed. Some primal possessive streak stirred in her belly and shot adrenaline through her blood. She wanted to hiss and spit and claw. Only a tiny thread of civility kept her from acting out some primitive vengeance.

When she could endure it no longer, she pushed back her chair, took a deep breath, and stood. Operating on the slim hope that he was engaged in some clandestine Ranger business, she fluffed her hair, stuck out her chest, and sauntered over to the two of them.

She ignored the redhead chewing on Holt's ear and brushed herself against his other side. "Hello, cowboy," she said in a breathless imitation of Mae West. "I like your equipment." Her hand drew lazy circles over his back, then slipped lower and pinched his bottom.

That got his attention.

Leaning over his shoulder, she nuzzled his cheek and whispered, "Are you undercover?"

His white teeth flashed in a seductive smile. "Not yet, li'l darlin', but I could be persuaded to get under the covers with you quicker than greased lightning."

She clenched her molars, curved her lips in a mock smile, and spoke in a low voice. "If you value your male anatomy, you snake, you'll get rid of that bimbo right now. I have a few things to say to you. And they're better said in private."

"Who the hell are you to be horning in on my man?" the redhead asked.

"Now, now, pretty ladies," he drawled, throwing an arm around each of them, "there's enough of me to go around."

Cory almost went through the ceiling. She hissed a string of colorful invectives in his ear that raised his eyebrows a foot.

"Hooo-wee." He grinned. "Yes, ma'am, that sounds real interesting." He turned to the redhead and said, "It's been nice spending time with you, Rusty, but I've got a little business to tend to with this lady."

Rusty grumbled and shot Cory a look that would split an atom, but she grabbed her drink and moved down the bar.

He swiveled on the stool and drew Cory between his long legs. "Sugar, I get the distinct impression that you're a little ticked off at me for some reason."

"Give the man a dollar knife." Sarcasm oozed from her words and fury pounded her pulsebeat. She was only half an inch away from making a horrendously embarrassing scene in a public place.

He shoved his hat back and scratched his head. "Did I do something to set you off?"

"Did you *do* something?" She sputtered with rage. "Holt Berringer, you are without a doubt the lowest, slimiest, sorriest—"

"Cory?"

"What?" she snapped.

He threw back his head and laughed.

She whopped him on the shoulder. "How dare you laugh at me, you pea-brained moose! You are lower than worm dirt!" Tears gathered in her eyes, but she willed them away. "Do you have any idea how badly you've hurt me? I could kill you. In fact, I think I will kill you, slowly and painfully—as soon as I can think of something nasty and awful enough."

His face softened. "Darlin', it would almost be worth dying to feel all that passion aimed at me. But I'm afraid you've got the wrong man."

Nine

Cory's eyes narrowed. "What do you mean 'the wrong man'? I've been sitting over there for twenty minutes watching you come on to that red-haired floozy like a stallion in heat."

He grinned. "She was doing most of the coming on. I was just sitting here, minding my own business, having a beer, and waiting for my brother, Holt."

"Your . . . brother?"

He nodded.

Surely, this was a joke, Cory thought. Holt had two brothers, but he'd never mentioned—"You're . . . *twins*?"

"Identical. I'm Ross."

A terrible sinking feeling washed over her as all sorts of embarrassing memories flitted through her head. A blush flared upward from her throat and heated her face to blazing scarlet. "Have you ever wished that the floor would open up and swallow you?"

He chuckled. "A few times." He glanced behind her toward the door. "Here comes Holt now."

Dropping her face in her hands, Cory groaned. "I may die of mortification. He'll never let me hear the end of this."

Ross leaned close and whispered in her ear. "If you'll take back that part about gelding me with an oyster shucker, we'll pretend the rest never happened."

"You've got a deal."

Ross straightened. "Uh-oh, big brother looks like his tail's on fire."

"What in the hell do you think you're doing, Ross?" Holt growled. "Get your hands off my woman."

Ross gave him a wide-eyed innocent look. "We were just getting acquainted."

"Well, get acquainted with your hands in your pockets." Holt pulled Cory to his side and kissed her temple. "Hi, babe. What are you doing here?"

"I got busy and skipped lunch, so I came in for a bite to eat. When I saw Ross, I . . . uh, thought it was you." She lifted her chin indignantly. "You didn't tell me you had a twin."

"Didn't I? Well," he said, grinning and playfully punching Ross's shoulder, "sometimes I like to forget about this rascal." He hugged her close, smiling down at her. "Where have you been? I've been trying to get hold of you all day."

Her finger twisted the hem of her top. "I've been at your house." She fluttered her hand toward the satchel by the window table. "Deciding about paint, wallpaper, carpet."

His smile faded. "Who went with you?"

"Nobody."

"Dammit, Cory! I told you not to go anywhere by yourself!"

"And I told *you*, Holt Berringer, I go where I please, when I please." She poked her finger against his chest and glared up at him. "Don't you start in on me. I've had a bad day."

Ross snorted with laughter. "That's telling him how the cow ate the cabbage, honey."

Holt glared at his brother. "You stay out of this." His face softened as he turned back to Cory. "Kitten, I'm sorry you've had a bad day, and I don't mean to fuss at you, but it scares the hell out of me to know you've been alone. It's dangerous."

Her shoulders slumped and she sighed with exasperation. "Oh, Holt, for goodness sakes, can't we give up this pretense? I figured out a long time ago that I'm no longer in danger. Warren Sikes is drinking tequila in Mexico."

"Maybe not."

Startled, she looked up at him. "What do you mean?"

"Last night a man held up a grocery store in Boerne, a little town a few miles northwest of San Antonio. He wore a Halloween mask and limped."

"You think it was Pig-face?"

"Could be. I don't want to take any chances. That's why Ross is here." He ran his thumb along the curve of her bottom lip. "Babe, as bad as I hate to, I've got to be out of town for a day or two, and when it gets right down to the nut cuttin', Ross is the only person I'd trust with your life."

"Where are you going?" she asked.

He cocked his head, and his lips twitched into a teasing smile. "Now, you know better than that."

"Okay, okay." She rolled her eyes, leaned over, and said to Ross in an undertone, "Big secret Ranger goings-on."

The men laughed, then Holt said, "Ross is a Texas Ranger too."

"Do you tote a gun, wear a silver star, and the whole schmear?"

"Yes, ma'am." Ross flashed the star pinned under his vest and grinned. "I'm tougher than a two-bit steak and proud to be one of those fellows that are in the right and keep on a-comin'."

She shook her head. "I can't get over how much you two not only look alike, but talk alike. It's amazing."

"There are a few differences," Ross said, winking. "He's the serious one; I'm a lot more fun. As soon as we get old Hoss out of the way, we'll kick up our heels and cut a rusty."

She cocked an eyebrow. "Am I going to have to get out my oyster shucker?"

Ross threw back his head and hooted with laughter. "I like this one, Hoss. She doesn't take a backseat to anybody."

Holt gathered her against his side, obviously pleased with his twin's approval of her. "What's this about an oyster shucker?"

"Private joke," she said. "When are you leaving?"

"Tonight. Are you going to miss me?"

She frowned. "Can Ross cook?"

"Not worth a damn."

She heaved a theatrical sigh. "Then I suppose I'm going to miss you."

• • •

And she did miss him. More than she thought possible after only one day.

Wednesday night, while she and Ross had dinner at a Sixth Street restaurant, she studied the man across the table. Ross looked like Holt and talked like Holt, but he wasn't Holt. His shoulders were as broad, his hair curled the same way, his smile was almost identical, but he didn't set her heart pounding and her blood racing. He didn't excite her senses and turn her knees to noodles. Not like Holt did. She sighed.

"You missing Hoss?"

She looked up from the steak she'd been sawing on without paying attention and nodded.

"He ought to be back tonight or tomorrow," Ross said.

"I'm sorry that you had to get dragged into this mess. I doubt that I'm in any real danger,"

"There wasn't much going on in Waco, and I had some time off coming. Hoss will rest easier if I'm here with you. He's head over heels about you, you know. I've never seen him so crazy about a woman before."

"But I thought he was engaged once."

"Mary Ann? I think she was a habit more than anything else. Never did like the woman. She was about as exciting as pig tracks."

Pressing her lips together, Cory tried not to giggle, but the sound escaped in spite of her efforts. "Pig tracks?"

He grinned. "Yeah. And that's giving her the benefit of the doubt. I guess having the mama that we do has spoiled us. Hoss and I need women with a little more spirit. I'm just damned sorry that he saw you first."

She smiled, happy with his approval. Why it seemed important, though, she couldn't fathom. Soon she'd be gone and she doubted if she'd ever see the Berringer brothers again. Uncomfortable with the twinge of pain she felt at that thought, she asked, "Why do you call him Hoss?"

"Has he told you who we were named after?"

"Your grandfather, Holt Ross." She smiled and added, "Another Texas Ranger."

"Yep. It was confusing having two Holts, so Grandpa started calling him Hoss. Since it rhymed with Ross and we're twins, it stuck. Neither he nor our mother ever liked it very much. I don't think anybody but me calls him that anymore. Say, you want some dessert?"

Cory declined, and after Ross had a big slab of cherry cheesecake, they decided to catch Sid's act at the comedy club. Even though Ross wasn't Holt, he was funny and charming, and she enjoyed his company.

And while Ross seemed loose and laid back, she noticed that his dark eyes were always moving. His hand was never far from his gun, and he stayed close to her.

Back on the street after the show, he asked, "What next, pretty lady?" He held up his arms and wiggled his rear. "Wanna go somewhere to sip a brew and boogie?"

Smiling broadly, she said, "You're on. Have you ever had a Molten Lava from the Fiery Furnace?"

"No, can't say as I have. I once got my butt

sunburned in Matamoros, though. Hurt like hell."

She burst into laughter. "Molten Lava is a drink, and the Fiery Furnace is a place." She grabbed him by the arm. "Come on. You're in for a treat."

In front of his club, Shadrach, dressed in his usual atrocious garb and with his hair in frizzy disarray, stood by the curb hustling patrons. When he saw her, his gap-toothed smile flashed and he grabbed her in his thick, dragon-embellished arms. "Hot damn, little mama," he bellowed, laughing and swinging her around. "How's tricks?"

"Set her down, buddy. Easy like." All frivolity had fled from Ross's voice. "Or I'm gonna open a big hole in your guts."

Her feet slid to the ground. Shad frowned. "What the hell's wrong with you, Holt? You know I'm not going to hurt Cory. We've played this scene before."

Cory tugged on Ross's arm. "Put your gun away," she whispered. "He's a friend." To Shad, she explained, "This isn't Holt, it's his twin brother. Shad Shapiro, Ross Berringer."

"Well, I'll be damned!" Shad pumped Ross's hand and thumped him on the back. "You had me fooled. Come on in and have a drink on the house." He threw a beefy arm around each of them and pulled them inside the noisy black cavern.

After her eyes had adjusted to the dark, smoky room, Cory spotted Roscoe, Mugger, and Dimples nursing beers with several other bikers.

"How's it going, Cory?" Dimples called.

She gave a thumbs-up sign and waved to the others.

Shad led them to a table in the corner, and Marcia, who was surprised to discover that Holt had a clone, chatted with them for a few minutes before taking their order.

"Nice folks," Ross said, his hand patting the table to the beat of the deafening rock music.

"I think so."

"Wanna dance?"

"I'd love it."

On the floor, Ross paused, shoved his hat back, then swung into loose-hipped gyrations as he moved to the rock beat. Cory joined him, amazed at his skill as a dancer. They laughed and cavorted through three songs before Cory begged a halt to cool off.

"I can't remember when I've had so much fun at a club," she said. "I love to dance."

Ross swigged a slug of the beer he'd opted for, then frowned. "What do you and Hoss usually do?"

She grinned.

"Besides that," he said.

"Oh, lots of things. We go to art exhibits and museums. He took me to a poetry reading the other night."

Ross sputtered into his beer. "A *poetry* reading? Jeez. Sounds worse than a dose of salts. Doesn't Holt take you dancing?"

She shook her head. "I *enjoyed* the poetry reading, and I thought maybe he didn't dance."

"Hoss?" Ross hooted. "He can dance rings around me." He leaned forward and cocked a teasing, smug smirk. "And I'm damned good."

"Modest too." Her straw slurped the bottom of

her Molten Lava, and she motioned to Marcia for another.

Eager to see Cory, Holt took the apartment steps two at a time, his boots clattering on the wooden stairs.

The apartment was empty.

"Damn!" He'd driven hell for leather from San Antonio to get back. Where were they? It was eleven o'clock. Had something happened? His mouth went dry and his heart pounded against his chest.

Maybe Shad knew something.

Three minutes later, Holt, nostrils flaring, stood at the bar glaring at Ross and Cory on the dance floor. They were both laughing as she twitched her tail like a mare at breeding time. Jealousy rose up in him and floated in front of his eyes like slime-green scum. He clenched his teeth and grabbed a beer off Marcia's tray.

"Oh, hi, Holt," she said. "You are Holt?"

"I am."

She cocked her head toward the dance floor. "You going to take over now?"

He tugged his hat low on his brow. "I am."

"I'm cutting in. Get lost, Ross."

"Hey, Hoss. Glad to see you back."

"I'll bet. Get lost."

As Ross left, Holt draped his arms on Cory's shoulders, his body swaying to the music. He smiled down at her, and she went weak all over. "I missed you, babe."

"I missed you too."

He gave her a quick peck, then stepped back and began to swivel his hips to the soft rock beat. She laughed and matched his moves. His eyes locked with hers as his movements became sheer seduction. Their awareness of others on the floor faded. The place faded. There was only one man and one woman and passion-stirring rhythm. Like native dancers in a fertility rite, they teased each other with thrusting hips and rotating pelvises, with twitching shoulders and sensual smiles.

He danced closer and closer, brushing and rubbing her body, then retreating. A damp sheen broke out over her body. Her breasts swelled, and her nipples hardened; a throb pulsated low in her belly.

When the music ended, she watched him pull a deep breath of air into his lungs. He wanted her. She felt the vibration of his desire tingle and stroke her, and her breath caught with the power of it as she watched him struggle for control.

He threw an arm around her shoulders and led her from the floor. Her hand slid into his back pocket. He stopped and leaned down to give her a hungry, openmouthed kiss.

"Woman," he murmured against her lips, "you're something else. Why didn't you tell me you could dance like that?"

"You never asked."

"Know what I want to do to you right now?"

"Tell me."

He whispered in her ear, and heat flooded her.

"Hooo-wee!" Ross said when they reached the table. "For a while there, I thought I might have to call the fire department."

"I thought I told you to get lost," Holt said.

"Now, Hoss, is that any way to talk to your brother? And here I've been risking life and limb to watch over your lady."

Holt glared at him. "I'm back now. You can leave."

"But I just ordered another round."

Amused by their bickering, Cory said, "While you two boys work this out, I'm going to the ladies' room." She grabbed her purse and made a hasty exit.

A few minutes later, she was blotting her face with a paper towel and glanced up when the door opened. "Hi, Dimples."

"Honey, if you're not the luckiest gal in the world, I'll kiss a hog. I can't believe there are two of those good-looking devils. I guess God hated to waste the pattern on just one. If you want to toss one of them back, I'll catch him." She patted her straw-colored hair, which still needed a root touch-up, and flashed a deep-dimpled smile.

"Roscoe would break my kneecaps," Cory said.

Dimples giggled. "He is kind of possessive." She jiggled toward the single stall of the rest room. "Catch you later."

Smiling, Cory opened the door to leave. Her smile died; her eyes widened. She sucked in a gasp and slammed the door. "Ohmylord!" Terrified whimpers squeaked from her throat as she threw herself against the door and fumbled for the lock.

"What's the matter, honey?" Dimples asked.

"It's Pig-face! Warren Sikes, the man who threatened to kill me. He's standing in the hallway not two feet away. He must have seen me and followed me back here." She managed to turn the thumb button in the knob, but it wouldn't hold long. Neither would the hook latch attached high in the worn wood, but she fastened it anyway. "We've got to get out of here," she said, looking back at Dimples. "He probably has a gun. Will that window open?"

Dimples tried the window, throwing her considerable weight into the effort. "It won't budge. The damned thing's painted shut. I can't break the glass. There's nothing but boards nailed behind it."

The doorknob jiggled back and forth. "He's trying to get in," Cory whispered, her hands shaking.

"What a hell of a time for me to leave my shiv at home. Here let me hold the door. I'm stronger than you. Look for something to use as a weapon."

While Dimples braced her back against the door, Cory scurried around the small room looking for something, anything, to defend themselves from Sikes.

The door trembled with heavy thuds.

"Dammit, where are the Rangers when I need them?" Cory tucked a can of roach spray under her arm and grabbed the heavy lid off the toilet tank.

"Hurry! I can't hold it much longer."

Cory thrust the spray can at Dimples. "When I count to three, move away from the door." She plastered herself to the wall beside the door and hoisted the porcelain lid over her head.

"One . . . two . . . three."

Dimples jumped away. The door frame splintered and Sikes charged in, gun drawn.

Dimples squirted him in the face with bug spray. Cory crashed the tank lid over his head. Stunned, Sikes dropped the gun and crumpled.

"Watch it!" Dimples shouted. "He's not out."

Dimples sat on his back, and Cory bashed him again.

"Get some help!" Dimples said.

"I'm not leaving you. He's still wiggling and the gun's under him. Let's tie him up."

"With what?"

Cory searched her purse. All she could find was waxed dental floss.

"Try this. It's strong."

She started a long string from the box. Dimples yanked his arms behind his back and wound the floss around his wrists like a calf roper.

Cory dumped change from her coin purse and began feeding quarters into the condom machine.

When his arms were bound with dental floss and his ankles with prophylactics, they rolled the dazed man onto his back.

Cory picked up the gun and stuck it in the waistband of her slacks. She and Dimples grinned and slapped hands in a high five.

"Nice try, sucker," Cory sneered down at the groaning man on the floor.

With Dimples on her heels, she charged out of the ladies' room and strode to the table where Holt and Ross sat drinking beers.

She plunked the gun on the table. "In case you're interested, Warren Sikes is in the ladies' room."

Holt's chair crashed to the floor as he jumped up. "Holy hell, is he loose?"

Cory smirked at Dimples. "Not as long as the rubbers hold."

Ten

With Sikes safely locked in the pokey, Cory was free to come and go as she pleased without Holt grousing about danger. She used her freedom to full advantage. After rushing through her duties at Sixth Scents, which took only an hour or two each morning, she labored like a demon on Holt's house, even working late a few nights when he had "secret" Ranger business. Used to the hectic atmosphere of an ad agency, she found coordinating and supervising the various decorating tasks and vendors a piece of cake. Knowing that Howard Ellison might call at any time with "the" opportunity, she was eager for her project to be completed before she went to California.

She and Holt had spent the previous weekend scouting for furniture to fill out the pieces from the warehouse, and by Friday afternoon, less than two weeks after she started, the interior was finished and everything had been delivered.

When the last delivery truck left, she made a final inspection of the spacious house, straightening a picture here, fluffing a pillow there, savoring the faint smells of wallpaper paste and paint that lingered in the rooms. The kitchen had turned out exactly as she'd imagined, and the expansive living area was homey and perfect. The new chandelier in the dining room gleamed above the Queen Anne table. The bedrooms, except for draperies due the following week, were ready for company. Only a few extra touches—accessories that Holt could add later—were needed.

She was saving the finished product as a surprise for that weekend and had her fingers crossed that he would like it. Feeling a swell of pride with her accomplishment, she stood at the front door and took one last look before she hurried home to dress for the opera.

"Are you about ready?" Holt asked outside her bedroom door.

"Give me two minutes," Cory replied.

She clipped shoulder-brushing pearl strands to her ears and picked up the jacket to her evening suit. The pale pink satin confection had cost the earth, and she'd packed it with a Los Angeles soiree in mind. She hoped it was appropriate for the opera in Austin.

Ankle-length and formfitting, the strapless dress, with its intricate pearl beading at hem and bodice, was both chic and deliciously decadent. The fitted jacket she buttoned over it was long-sleeved with more pearl designs at the wrist, and the rolled collar bounded a deeply scooped neckline that skimmed her shoulders and dipped below the lustrous motif edging the bodice.

After adding lipstick and a tissue to her evening bag, she took a deep breath and left her bedroom.

"Wow!" Holt said when she entered the living room.

"Wow, yourself." Her gaze swept appreciatively over his evening attire and the man wearing it. Rather than looking out of place in a tuxedo, he wore the well-tailored outfit with a panache that told her he was no stranger to formal occasions. She smiled when she noted his footwear—black lizard boots.

His dark eyes gleamed like the onyx studs in his shirt. "Turn around," he said.

She made a slow revolution. "Am I okay?"

He gently batted one pearl earring and set it swinging against her bare shoulder, then kissed the places it brushed. "Perfect. Absolutely perfect. I'll be the envy of every man there."

She hugged him. "And every lady will have her eyes on you. You're very handsome this evening." Feeling no telltale bulge beneath his jacket, she patted under his arms and down his hips. "Did you forgo your gun for the occasion?"

"Now, babe, you know I feel naked without my gun. Want to frisk me again? Feels good."

She complied, lingering in a spot or two to tease him.

"A little lower. Lower. Ah, that's it."

"Holt Berringer, that's not a gun."

The corners of his mouth twitched. "Well, I suppose it's a matter of semantics."

"Okay, I give up. Where is it?"

"In the side of my boot. Ready, pretty lady?"

Downstairs at the entrance, a crowd had gathered. "What's going on?" she asked.

He gave her a secret smile. "Princess, your carriage awaits."

At the curb sat an open white carriage drawn by a huge Percheron. The frock-coated driver tipped his top hat, and Wee Willie rushed forward with a small nosegay of pink roses and baby's breath.

"Thanks, Willie." She held them to her nose and breathed in their sweet fragrance. "They're lovely."

"Hot damn, little mama, you're traveling in style tonight," Shad shouted from his spot in front of the Fiery Furnace. Marcia and several bikers had congregated with Shad and shot a thumbs-up.

Pleased by Holt's romantic touch, Cory smiled and kissed his cheek as he helped her into the blue velvet carriage seat. When the horse started down Sixth Street with a slow clop, she smiled and returned the waves of both strangers and the street regulars who were friends.

Holt put his arm around her and drew her against him. "Like the carriage?"

Delighted laughter bubbled from her lips as she snuggled close to him. "I love it. I feel a bit like Princess Di on her wedding day."

"I'll hire it again if you want to extend the imitation."

Feeling giddy, she laid her head on his shoulder, relishing his warmth and sharp masculine scent and absorbing the peacefulness of the relaxed Texas city.

Eventually, the carriage pulled to a stop in front

of the Paramount Theatre, a rather plain building amid the more ornate Victorian structures surrounding it, and Holt helped her down.

"Barbara has told me how beautifully the inside has been restored," Cory said. "I'm eager to see it."

"It was built around 1915 and has served as everything from a vaudeville palace to a movie theater," Holt said. "The new owners have done a fine job reviving it."

As they joined other formally dressed patrons entering the neoclassic auditorium, Cory's breath left her. Lushly and lovingly restored, the great arched ceiling of rich burgundy shone with prodigious amounts of heavily carved and gilded trim. Forest-green tapestry covered the walls, and in the ceiling near the stage was a grand circular painting of a musical goddess with flowing robes who fluttered her wings and plucked her harp above the orchestra pit.

"I feel as if we've stepped back in time," Cory whispered as they walked down the aisle to their seats.

For a moment the buzzing of conversation heightened, then ceased as the fire curtain lifted, and they were thrust into the rollicking gaiety of Seville.

Cory remained entranced until the last note died away and the curtain fell. Even after the applause subsided and they made their way to the exit, the music soared in her imagination. It stayed with her as they stepped into the waiting carriage.

"Oh, to be able to sing like that," she sighed to Holt as the horse clip-clopped down Congress Avenue.

He leaned close to her and sang in his low bass voice, "'Fig-a-ro, Fig-a-ro.'"

She snuggled close. "I think you show great promise—as a Texas Ranger."

"What?" he exclaimed in mock offense. "You don't want me to serenade you?"

She only laughed and settled into the crook of his arm, enjoying the bewitching ambience of the night and the full moon that added its light to the ornate street lamps lining the avenue.

As the carriage took them on a leisurely ride around the Capitol grounds, she said, "I can't believe that I've been here a month and never toured the Capitol."

"We'll put that on this weekend's agenda."

"And I've never been to your ranch."

"That's on next weekend's agenda."

"Will Ross be there?" she asked.

"Not if I can help it."

"I think you're jealous."

"Damned right." He nuzzled her ear.

"There's no need to be. It's the strangest thing. Even though he looks exactly like you, he doesn't turn me on."

"And I do?"

"Like a house afire." Her hand slid up his thigh.

"I wish this damned horse would hurry."

The moment her apartment door closed, he gathered her into his arms and brushed his lips across her temple. She melted as she did every time he touched her.

"That had to be the slowest blamed horse in

Texas," he said. He slipped off her jacket and tossed it on the back of a chair. His tongue teased a path along one bare shoulder. "I have champagne chilling. Why don't you slip out of the rest of that pretty dress before I'm tempted to rip it off? I'll meet you in the bedroom."

Powerful currents of desire jolted through her, and her fingers curled around his neck, threading through the soft hair at his nape. "I don't need champagne. I need you."

He smiled. "Don't worry your sweet little head about it, darlin', I mean for you to have both. As much as you want." He inched down the back zipper of her dress, then lightly swatted her bottom. "Scoot before I mess up my plans. I want to do this right."

She gave him a lusty smile and picked up her jacket. "You seem very mysterious. Are we celebrating something?"

"Not yet."

As she started to the bedroom, the phone rang. "I'll get it." She finished unzipping her dress as she hurried to pick up the receiver.

"Hello," she said, stepping out of her dress and tossing it on the bed.

"Cory Bright?"

"Yes?" She kicked off her shoes.

"This is Scott Swift of GSD&H in L.A. Are you familiar with our agency?"

Her heart tripped into maximum overdrive, and she sank to the mattress before her knees buckled. "Certainly, Mr. Swift. Your firm has an excellent reputation."

"I hope I'm not calling too late, but I've been trying to get you all evening."

"No, no, it's not too late. I've just come in from the opera." While she spoke, she slipped into a silk kimono and tied the sash with shaky fingers.

"An opera in Austin, Texas?"

She bit back a snappy rejoinder and chuckled instead. "They have quite an excellent company here."

"Cory, I've been hearing excellent things about *you*."

"Oh?"

"Howard Ellison sent me your résumé a few days ago, and Bill Flaherty mentioned your work with him when we had dinner last night in Atlanta."

"Bill is the dearest man. How is he?"

"Well enough to win all my money playing golf. And he said we'd be crazy not to snap you up before another agency beat us to it. Interested in an account executive spot on the coast with us? We can offer you a honey of a deal."

She squelched the urge to jump up and down and scream, "Yes! Yes!" Instead, she said calmly, "I'm open to the possibility."

"Let's talk. Can you fly out Sunday for a few days to meet some people? I know that's short notice, but we need to fill our spot quickly."

"I'm sure I can arrange it, Mr. Swift." She laughed at his comment and corrected herself. "Very well, Scott." She scribbled down the flight number and time. "Three oh two, L.A.X. . . . I'm looking forward to meeting you, too, Scott."

She hung up the receiver, thrust her hands in the air, and screamed, "Ya-hooo!" Noticing Holt leaning against the doorjamb, she ran to him, threw her arms around his neck, and gave him a loud smack. "Wipe that scowl off your face, Ranger, and open the champagne. I've got great news!"

"Who's Scott? And who the hell is Bill?"

"Scott Swift is a partner in GSD&H, only the hottest advertising agency in Los Angeles. And Bill Flaherty, that dear, dear sweet man, is my college roommate's father and a high-muckety-muck in Theta Airlines. My connection with Bill helped secure the Theta account for my old agency in Atlanta. Obviously, GSD&H is going after Theta's seventy-five-million-dollar business, and I'm to be part of the bait."

"Sounds like a sleazy deal to me."

"Don't knock it. That's the way the game is played. And I can deliver. Bill is like a second father to me, and I'm godmother to his only grandson. Hot damn!" She squeezed Holt again. "GSD&H! I'm on my way."

He frowned. "You're excited about this, aren't you?"

"Of course I'm excited. It's everything I've ever dreamed of. I'm going to rub a few noses in it."

"Don't you have to interview for the position first?"

She shrugged. "Oh, sure, but I suspect it will be only a formality. When they find out that I probably can bring Orianna Fragrances with me, too, by offering Mignon's formulas as an enticement, it's a done deal. For *big* bucks."

"Any chance you'll turn their proposition down?"

"Only for a *much* better one."

He took her hand. "Come with me. I may have a better proposition for you." He led her to his bedroom and opened the door.

Scores of small scented candles lit the room. Nestled in colored glass holders, they flickered everywhere—on the dresser, the chest, the wide headboard of the bed, the nightstand. Shimmering clusters of jewel-toned votives lit the corners and reflected from the mirror.

Soft music played, and on a small trunk at the foot of the bed sat a silver champagne bucket and two tulip glasses.

Tears filled Cory's eyes and she leaned back against him. "Oh, Holt. You did this for me?"

He brushed his cheek over the top of her head. "For you, babe."

She sniffled. "How romantic."

He sat her on the foot of the bed by the trunk and opened the champagne.

When she saw the label, her eyes widened. "Dom Perignon?"

"Only the best for you, princess." After he poured each of them a glass of the effervescent wine, he held his up in a toast. "To the woman I love with all my heart."

Her breath caught. "Holt, you've never said that before."

"What?"

"That you love me."

"Sure I have. Hundreds of times. I must have."

She shook her head.

"I meant to. I do love you, Cory." His thumb gently stroked her lower lip, then he reached into his pocket. "I tried to find some chocolate-covered strawberries, but I couldn't. Will this do?" He pulled out a cellophane-wrapped Moon Pie with a red ribbon tied around the middle.

She wiped away tears and laughed as she reached for it. A fiery sparkle in the center of the bow caught her eye and she looked closer. "It's a—a—"

"A ring." He untied the ribbon and slipped the huge diamond on her finger. "Cory, will you marry me?"

She gasped, then gulped some wine. "Marry you? But I never dreamed you'd ask me to marry you."

He knelt beside her. "Honey, I love you. I want to marry you and have kids and watch sunsets while we grow old together. Don't you love me?"

With his face turned up to hers and candlelight flickering in his black eyes, never had Holt Berringer looked so dear, so vulnerable. Her heart swelled and a tremendous tenderness washed over her. She leaned forward and kissed him. "Yes, I love you."

He stood and drew her to him. Between sips of champagne they kissed—lips, eyes, cheeks, noses, chins—until their glasses were emptied and set aside. They undressed each other slowly, and his mouth and hands were all over her, kissing her with lips scented with wine and caressing her with fingers that stoked her to eager trembling.

He laid her on the bed and, his face filled with love, whispered endearments and praise of her hair, her body, her face. Before she could speak her needs, he seemed to know them. It was heaven. Her breasts ached; he cupped them and laved them with his tongue. Her skin tingled; his hands glided across every bare inch of her body. Her back arched; he turned her to her side and nibbled a sensual path up her spine until she burned for him.

She shifted and pulled him to her, reveling in the touch of his chest against her breasts, his cheek, faintly rough with stubble, against hers. Her fingers, greedy and demanding, dug into his taut buttocks. He laughed softly and moved into the cradle of her legs, then entered her with maddening slowness.

Boundaries dissolved, and they merged and moved as one entity. "God, I love you."

With a savage male growl, he changed the tempo of their joining to one of fierce possession. His eyes closed and his teeth clenched, he drove with mounting ferocity. The muscles of his back rippled under her fingers as he lifted her, claimed her, swamped her with devouring fervor. On fire and charged with wildness, she matched him move for move, urging him on with her cries until their bodies were slick with sensual exertion and their breathing hot and hard.

Straining, straining, she held on to the earth with the tips of her fingers. Suddenly, she let go and was swept to the stars in a series of blinding, shattering spasms. He cried out and followed her in a climax that bowed his back and contorted his face with its potency.

She stroked his back and his buttocks, gentling him with touches and words. After a few moments, he rolled away and drew her against him, caressing the curve of her hip.

"Every time we make love," he said, "I think that it can't get any better. But it does. Woman, you'll wear me out by the time I'm forty."

She drew a lazy circle through a whorl of dark hair on his chest. "I doubt that."

He picked up her hand and studied the large diamond that shimmered with glittering fire in the candlelight. "I like having my ring on your finger. It tells the world you're mine. When can we get married? If it's okay with you, I'd like to make it soon. How about tomorrow?"

She laughed. "I think we need to discuss some things first."

"Like what?"

"Like where we'll live."

"You don't like my house?"

"You know I *love* your house. Haven't I been running myself ragged decorating it? But if we were to get married, would you consider moving to California?"

"Babe, a Texas Ranger's territory doesn't extend beyond El Paso."

"But if I take the account exec job with GSD&H, I'll be moving to L.A."

"Kitten, if you marry me, you won't need the job in L.A. I know nobody can live very high on the hog on a Ranger's pay, but I have some other assets. I have money coming in from the family business—mostly from insurance and banking. And the ranch that Ross and I have covers several thousand acres. Half of it's full of cattle and the other half is full of oil wells. We won't starve."

She raised up and looked at him. "You *are* rich."

He shrugged. "Some might say."

"Well, that simplifies things. You don't need to stay with the Rangers. You could resign and come to California with me."

"No, babe, I couldn't. I'll be a Ranger until I die or until I'm forced to retire. Being a Texas Ranger is bred in my bones. It's my dream come true. It's what *I am.*"

"My job will be in L.A. This opportunity is what I've always dreamed of. An account executive in the top ad agency in the country. It's what *I* am."

"But darlin'," he said, stroking her hair back from her face, "it's different for a woman."

Cory's spine went poker-stiff and her eyes spewed sparks. She shot up out of the bed. "Damn you, Holt Berringer!" She tore the ring off her finger and hurled it at him. "Damn your red-necked, chauvinistic hide to hell!"

Eleven

The long flight to Los Angeles gave Cory time to think. More than enough time. Her arguments with Holt chased around and around in her head. They were at an impasse, and all because of his damned masculine pride and stubbornness. She'd known better than to become involved with such a man. Hadn't she warned herself dozens of times? But did she listen to her own sage advice? No.

She'd allowed herself to be convinced that he was different from the typical macho stereotype, but, when push came to shove, machismo reared its ugly head and roared. He was a *Texas Ranger.* Well, he could stay in Texas and be a Ranger. Why should *she* be the one to forsake her career, her dream? Because she was a woman? Humph!

All day Saturday, they had chewed the subject to death. They had discussed, debated, argued. They had each hinted, cajoled, pleaded, and begged to no avail. They had explored compromises and concessions without success. She was going to California; he was staying in Texas.

Even though they tried to declare periods of truce to enjoy their time together, their mood put a damper on her surprise of having the house finished. They spent Saturday afternoon at the Old Pecan Street Art Festival, watching jugglers and fire-eaters and street musicians. They visited booths and ate cotton candy and acted with forced gaiety until tension and exhaustion forced them to her apartment. There they made love with fierce desperation.

In the end, nothing was resolved. He packed when she did.

Damn Holt Berringer's sexy black eyes! she thought as the plane descended into L.A. He could rot in Texas for all she cared!

Cory held her purse close as she made her way through the jostling, rushing crowd at L.A.X. to claim her luggage. The instant she stepped outside the sprawling terminal, fumes assaulted her. Car fumes, bus fumes, noxious exhaust smells hung in the gold-tinged haze that hovered over the city. People shouted in a dozen languages and rushed around like piranhas in a feeding frenzy. Group leaders waved signs and herded startled-looking tourists into waiting buses that belched still more noise and fumes into the atmosphere. The whole scene set her temples pounding.

A moment of agoraphobic panic seized her as she scanned a long row of limos lining the curb. When she saw a driver standing beside a white stretch Cadillac with her name on his placard, her spirits lifted. Now this was the way to go.

Even from her protected pocket in the limo, though, Cory felt the frenetic pace of the city press in on her as they drove down La Cienega and jockeyed into the freeway swarm. As teeming as the thoroughfares were on Sunday afternoon, she could only imagine the bumper-to-bumper frustration of weekday rush hour. Although she'd been to Los Angeles several times on business, she'd forgotten the frantic tempo of the city. And that everything was so crowded. There was no sense of space or breathing room. Austin, it was not.

When the chauffeured car turned into the lush, exotically landscaped grounds of the hotel, her tension ebbed. A peaceful, cloistered aura encompassed the huge Beverly Hills Hotel, where she was whisked inside the elegantly restored pink landmark by a deferential staff.

A smiling clerk welcomed her. "Miss Bright, a message for you." He held out a vellum envelope.

Holt! she thought with a rush of joy. Forsaking all the decorum appropriate to her chic surroundings, she ripped open the envelope. Her smile waned when she saw Scott Swift's name. It was a note welcoming her to L.A. and inviting her to an informal party in Malibu that evening.

Flowers from the agency and a tray of fruit and canapés waited in her lavish suite. She smelled the tropical arrangement of exotic ginger and anthuriums and nibbled a melon wedge. After she'd sent her clothes to be pressed, she drew a bath in a sumptuous room complete with bidet and crystal chandelier.

Lolling in the sunken tub amid a mound of bubbles, she lifted her leg and wiggled her toes through the scented froth. "Not bad for a gal from Goat Hill, Arkansas."

The sun was fading into the Pacific as Scott Swift's black Lamborghini roared through Malibu. Cory was pleased Scott seemed to approve of her already, but she was disappointed in the sunset. The gaudiness and clutter of the community encroached on the horizon and marred the sight. Vendors hawked beach towels, balloons, and general sleaze. Boisterous beach people, loud and high on the Lord only knew what, hurried to have a good time and squeeze the final hours from their weekends. A frenetic and plastic feel overlaid the area.

The gated and guarded section that the sports car turned into was a marked contrast to the garish commercialism. The air reeked money. This was the Malibu bastion of the rich and famous.

Inside the sprawling beach home that belonged to Kiki and Sam Goodman—the G of GSD&H—high-pitched laughter and the clink of ice cubes punctuated the sounds of a live trio playing in a corner somewhere in the open, starkly elegant rooms.

"Oh, darling, we're so glad you could come," her hostess said, kissing the air beside her cheek. Kiki, a tanned, fortyish blonde in silk hostess pajamas, looked like she starved herself every other day.

Sam gave her a faintly lecherous smile and held her hand a little too long. "We've heard some fantastic things about you, Cory. Help yourselves to a drink and, Scott, introduce our lady around."

After they stopped by the bar for a spritzer for Cory and a Scotch for Scott, they circulated among the crowd. She met the D&H of the agency and their wives, a movie producer who lived next door and his miniskirted third wife who'd been a Miss October in *Playboy*, a slightly anemic young sculptor in coveralls whose work was the current rage, a few others from the agency, and assorted clients from major accounts.

As a person who genuinely enjoyed people, Cory had no difficulty with small talk, so Scott left her on her own and wandered away to hustle Miss October. Yet after an hour or so, she discovered that she was growing bored with the "on" personae of the tanned, gaunt, silk-clad women and the Type A men who seemed to define themselves by money and power. The whole bunch, who darted around and gesticulated like speed freaks, seemed insincere and silly. Their clipped, acronym-laden speech, the name-dropping, the phoniness gave her a headache. Was this life in the fast lane?

Perhaps she was tired. Perhaps she needed time to adjust to the culture shock, she told herself. But after another fifteen minutes, she escaped to the powder room to keep from screaming.

Her escape attempt was futile. A pair of tanned women with tight-stretched faces and bony frames were there, adding another layer of lipstick and discussing lunch on Friday at the Bistro and the success of their latest liposuctions.

Liposuctions? Cory thought. Compared to those two, her own size eight seemed gargantuan. She smiled at them, blotted her face with a tissue, and spritzed herself from a spray flacon of her perfume.

"Dahling, what a divine fragrance," Mrs. H, one of the gaunt, recarved duo, exclaimed. "What *is* it?"

"A custom blend. My godmother formulated it for me. She was a perfumer until she retired recently."

"Would we recognize her name?"

Something about Mrs. H's supercilious tone rankled Cory. Her eyebrows and her nose lifted a fraction. "Perhaps. She is Mignon Marseau."

"Ah, French?"

Via Goat Hill, Arkansas, and Austin, Texas. "Yes. I'm sure you're familiar with Marseau wines."

"But of course." Mrs. H's eyes brightened.

"And she's your godmother?" the other woman asked.

Their interest in her was suddenly piqued, and Cory found herself with two new gushing friends and an invitation to lunch. Oh, joy.

On Tuesday morning, Cory clung to the seat while her maniacal taxi driver wove through legions of British, French, and German luxury cars converging on downtown L.A. like ants to a sugar spill. Their destination was the financial center where a great cluster of skyscrapers soared above the city in a modern version of temples to a god. Disciples and supplicants in business attire, some conservative, some totally avant-garde, clutched their briefcases and portfolios and scurried toward their respective temples like actors in a fast-forward movie.

After her driver was paid and tipped, Cory straightened the Hermes scarf at the neck of her beige linen coatdress and charged into the fray.

GSD&H occupied several floors of a lofty glass edifice protruding into the gray-gold haze. Cory went to the twenty-third floor.

She'd spent the day before familiarizing herself with the high-tech, energetic agency. Mark Davenport, a slick account executive in an Armani suit, had acted as tour guide and propagandist. He'd used a lot of words like fast track, high visibility, hot, and power. She'd had lunch at a "high visibility" in-spot with several of the account group members. The whole thing had reminded her of sorority rush week.

She wondered if they really wanted her or the Theta account. Maybe Mrs. H was pressuring Mr. H, hoping that Cory would give her a quart of her custom-blended perfume if she were hired.

Scott Swift's secretary gave her a broad smile and escorted her into the boss's office.

"Lunch at the Polo Lounge on Thursday, Bob," Scott was saying into his phone. "You've got it." He hung up and rose to meet Cory. "What do you think of our operation?"

"I'm very impressed."

"And we're impressed with you, Cory. We'd like for you to be part of our team." He named a salary figure that stunned her, though she tried to mask her reaction. "Of course, that doesn't include bonuses," he added, then lifted his brows, awaiting her response.

"I'll need some time to think about it. A few days."

"We'd like to move on this quickly, Cory." He leaned forward and flashed a conspiratorial smile. "We could sweeten the kitty by another ten thou."

She almost swallowed her tongue.

"What do you say?"

The niggling headache that had plagued her since Sunday erupted full force. She rubbed her temples. "I'll give you an answer in the morning."

Why was she stalling? she wondered. Everything she'd always wanted was being offered to her on a silver platter. It made no sense, but with her head pounding, she couldn't think.

After two aspirins and a long soak in the tub, Cory sat on the couch in her suite with her arms hugging her knees. Her headache had abated, and she'd had lots of time to think rationally. The bare facts were that she hated L.A. She hated the high-stress pace, the crowding, the smog. And the people at GSD&H were a pain in the caboose.

If she were totally honest with herself, she'd admit that she didn't want the position. She didn't want to be a slick hustler for the agency. What she had always wanted was to prove that she was a talented and worthwhile woman who could succeed on individual merit. She'd done that. GSD&H really wanted her, and the salary they'd offered was four times the amount any of her brothers earned. She'd won the race; she didn't need a medal to prove it. Besides, races weren't all that important anyway.

But what was important?

She rang the doorbell a second time and waited on the dark porch. The night air was clean and fresh, and tree frogs chirred through the stillness.

The door opened and Holt's large frame filled the entrance. His hair was rumpled, his shirttail was pulled out of his jeans, and he wore only socks on his feet. "Cory?"

She laughed. "Have I changed that much in three days?"

"You haven't changed at all, kitten. You're a sight for sore eyes." He glanced down at the luggage by her feet. "You didn't get the job?"

"Oh, but I did. At least, it was offered to me. I turned them down."

"Why?"

"For lots of reasons. If you'll invite me in, I'll tell you all about it."

"*Mi casa, su casa*, babe." He picked up her cases and stepped back for her to enter. When the door closed, he dropped the luggage and gathered her in his arms. "Dear Lord, I've missed you."

She held on tight. "I've missed you too." She leaned back to gaze up into his face. "I decided that California without you would be terribly boring. I absolutely *hated* the place."

With effort, he held back a triumphant grin. He had to be sure. "Are you back for good?"

"That depends."

"On what?"

"Is your offer for having kids and watching sunsets and growing old together still open?"

That triumphant grin broke forth. "You betcha."

"Then I'm back for good."

He held her close, the misery of the past four days rolling away. He would have waited years for her. "What happened to your dream of being an account executive with a big advertising agency?"

"The important thing is that I love you, Holt. And a dream without you is a nightmare. I'll tell you all the rest later. Much later." She curled her fingers around his neck and drew his mouth to hers in a searing, hungry kiss.

"Later," he agreed when he came up for air. "I love you, Cory. Remind me to tell you at least twice a day for the rest of our lives." He scooped her into his arms and carried her upstairs to the master bedroom.

"I see that the drapes were delivered," she said as he unbuttoned her blouse.

"Uh-huh," he replied as he nibbled her neck and unzipped her slacks. "Came today."

"You like the"—she squealed as his tongue invaded her ear—"color?"

"Uh-huh. They're blue—like your eyes."

"Look again."

He chuckled and his belt buckle hit the floor.

THE EDITOR'S CORNER

It's going to be a merry month, indeed, for all of us LOVESWEPT devotees with romances that are charming, delightful, moving, and hot!

First, one of Deborah Smith's most romantic, dreamy love stories ever, CAMELOT, LOVESWEPT #468. Deb sweeps you away to sultry Florida, a setting guaranteed to inspire as much fantasizing in you as it does in heroine Agnes Hamilton. The story opens on a stormy night when Agnes has been thinking and dreaming about the love story recorded in the diary of a knight of Britain's Middle Ages. He seems almost real to her. When the horses on her breeding farm need her help to shelter from the wind and rain, Agnes forges out into the night—only to meet a man on horseback who seems for all the world like her knight of old. Who is the wickedly handsome John Bartholomew and dare she trust their instant attraction to each other? This is a LOVESWEPT to read slowly so you can enjoy each delicious phrase of a beautiful, sensual, exciting story.

Welcome a marvelous new talent to our fold, Virginia Leigh, whose SECRET KEEPER, LOVESWEPT #469, is her first published novel. Heroine Mallory Bennett is beautiful, sexy—and looking her worst in mud-spattered jeans (sounds like real life, huh?), when hero Jake Gallegher spots her in the lobby of his restaurant. From the first he knows she's Trouble . . . and he senses a deep mystery about her. Intrigued, he sets out to probe her secrets and find the way to her heart. Don't miss this moving and thrilling love story by one of our New Faces of '91!

Joan Elliott Pickart is back with a funny, tender, sizzler, MEMORIES, LOVESWEPT #470. This is an irresistible story of a second chance at love for Minty Westerly and Chism Talbert. Minty grew up happy and privileged;

Chism grew up troubled and the caretaker's son. But status and money couldn't come between them for they had all the optimism of the young in love. Then Chism broke Minty's heart, disappearing on the same night they were to elope. Now, back in town, no longer an angry young man, but still full of passion, Chism encounters Minty, a woman made cautious by his betrayal. Their reunion is explosive—full of pain and undimmed passion . . . and real love. You'll revel in the steps this marvelous couple takes along the path to true love!

That marvelous romantic Linda Cajio gives you her best in EARTH ANGEL, LOVESWEPT #471, next month. Heroine Catherine Wagner is a lady with a lot on her mind—rescuing her family business from a ruthless and greedy relative while pursuing the cause of her life. When she meets charismatic banker Miles Kitteridge she thinks he must be too good to be true. His touch, his fleeting kisses leave her weak-kneed. But is he on to her game? And, if so, can she trust him? Miles knows he wants the passionate rebel in his arms forever . . . but capturing her may be the toughest job of his life! A real winner from Linda!

Welcome another one of our fabulous New Faces of '91, Theresa Gladden, with her utterly charming debut novel, ROMANCING SUSAN, LOVESWEPT #472. First, devastatingly handsome Matt Martinelli steals Susan Wright's parking space—then he seems determined to steal her heart! And Susan fears she's just going to be a pushover for his knock-'em-dead grin and gypsy eyes. She resists his lures . . . but when he gains an ally in her matchmaking great aunt, Susan's in trouble—delightfully so. A love story of soft Southern nights and sweet romancing that you'll long remember!

Patt Bucheister strikes again with one of her best ever sensual charmers, HOT PURSUIT, LOVESWEPT #473. Rugged he-man Denver Sierra is every woman's dream and a man who will not take no for an answer. Lucky Courtney Caine! But it takes her a while to realize just how lucky she is. Courtney has hidden in the peaceful shadows cast by her performing family. Denver is determined to draw her out into the bright sunshine of life . . . and to melt her icy fears with the warmth of his affection and the fire of his desire. Bravo, Patt!

We trust that as always you'll find just the romances you want in all six of our LOVESWEPTs next month. Don't forget our new imprint, FANFARE, if you want more of the very best in women's popular fiction. On sale next month from FANFARE are three marvelous novels that we guarantee will keep you riveted. MORTAL SINS is a mesmerizing contemporary novel of family secrets, love, and unforgettable intrigue from a dynamic writing duo, Dianne Edouard and Sandra Ware. THE SCHEMERS by Lois Wolfe is a rich, thrilling historical novel set during the Civil War with the most unlikely—and marvelous—heroine and hero. She's a British aristocrat, he's a half-Apache army scout. Be sure also to put Joan Dial's sweeping historical FROM A FAR COUNTRY on your list of must-buy fiction. This enthralling novel will take you on a romantic journey between continents . . . and the hearts and souls of its unforgettable characters.

Ah, so much for you to look forward to in the merry month ahead.

Warm good wishes,

Carolyn Nichols

Carolyn Nichols
Editor
LOVESWEPT
Bantam Books
666 Fifth Avenue
New York, NY 10102-0023